Christmas in Newfoundland
Memories and Mysteries

Christmas in Newfoundland

Memories  Mysteries

A
SGT. WINDFLOWER
BOOK

MIKE MARTIN

OTTAWA
PRESS AND
PUBLISHING

ottawapressandpublishing.com

Copyright © Mike Martin 2019

ISBN (pbk.) 978-1-988437-25-5
ISBN (EPUB) 978-1-988437-27-9
ISBN (MOBI) 978-1-988437-26-2

Design and composition:
Magdalene Carson / New Leaf Publication Design

This is a work of fiction. All of the characters, names, incidents,
organizations, and dialogue in this novel are either products of the
author's imagination or are used fictitiously.

To Ted and Jane
and memories of Christmas past.

To Sophie, Ruby, Nolan and Rebecca
and Christmas yet to come.

Contents

Acknowledgements

Many thanks to Publisher Ron Corbett from Ottawa Press and Publishing and Magdalene Carson of New Leaf Publication Design who did such a great job of putting this book together. A special thank you to Bernadette Cox who shaped and edited the raw stories into what we hope will be an enjoyable peek into Christmas of today and yesterday.

The illustrations in this book came from a very talented group of young artists from the Visual Arts Program at Canterbury High School in Ottawa. They read the stories and under the guidance of their teacher, Christos Pantieras, came up with their interpretation of the stories as they saw them. They competed for the right to be in this book and all of them should be congratulated for their individual and collective efforts. We hope you enjoy them, as we do, as much as the stories.

Introduction

Memories and Mysteries started when I was a child. The idea for the book began with stories told to me in my youth about Christmas in a long-ago Grand Bank, where gifts were few and love was plenty. Those were the days when the snow and a homemade sled were sufficient entertainment, the nights were filled with kerosene lamps and laughter, and the twelve days of Christmas were a time for family, friends and roving bands of mummers.

The stories then became about my own Christmas memories in the streets of St. John's in the 1960s. Water Street was the only place to shop. Stores like Ayre's and Bowring's and the Arcade held a young child in rapture with the toys in the windows as Christmas music blared everywhere, and a live turkey and a boy with a giant bell called shoppers to the Mount Cashel Raffle. There was always at least one night, too, spent on a hot, sticky bus to see the wondrous lights all over town.

The mysteries came much later, but just like me, the characters in the Sgt. Windflower Mysteries loved Christmas and the enduring traditions of caring and sharing that they found in Grand Bank. Windflower, Sheila and Eddie Tizzard all had new adventures across Christmastime each year. They found their way into trouble and back out again, always in time to enjoy the most magical time of the year.

I hope you enjoy reading these stories as much as I have enjoyed writing them. I wrote them initially as a way to celebrate Christmas with my family and friends. Now I offer them to you and yours. May the spirit of Christmas fill your hearts and may it last all year long.

Mike Martin
Author, Sgt. Windflower Mysteries.

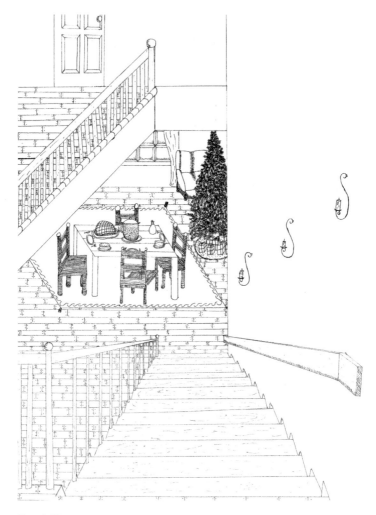

Farrah Munro

A Grand Bank Christmas

They are now in their seventies, slowing physically but sharp of mind and wit. Despite the twinkle in their eyes when asked what it was like growing up in Grand Bank, they seem reticent at first to open up about those days so long ago.

"Cold," he says when asked what winter was like, hoping this one-word answer will slow the questioning. But his partner decides more can be offered.

"Banks of snow," she says, "up to the rooftops."

"No, up to the tops of the fences," he counters.

Now the game is on, and she will not be slowed down. "Don't you remember we used to be over at old Mrs. Pike's after a snowfall, and we could climb up on top of the snow and look in through her bedroom window?"

And so it begins, this long slow stroll through winter and Christmas past in the small Town of Grand Bank, Newfoundland, home of adventure and the famous Grand Bank schooner, and for a ten-year-old boy and a nine-year-old girl, a world of magical white and wonder.

She was the studious one who lived across from the school and paid rapt attention to whatever the teacher presented. He lived half a block away and was more likely to spend most of his school day trying to distract the rest of the students from learning anything. He sat in front of her in class and would reach behind to try to grab her books.

"All you could see were these two big hands grabbing at you," she laughs.

They had travelled many different paths since those days, he to join the air force and travel the world, building family and friends along the way. She hadn't travelled as far, but the world of big city Toronto was oceans away from her way of life during her early Grand Bank days.

After nearly fifty years and each losing their life partners, they had found each other again on visits to their old home=town. Now a secure, happy and loving couple, they are united by a shared past and future together. They sit in the kitchen of his old house in Grand Bank, one that his grandfather had built by hand, and through numerous cups of strong black tea, they talk about what life was like in the way back when.

Winter was a sometimes bitter and hard season in old-time Grand Bank, even if they were slow to acknowledge it. There was no electricity, no central heating and no indoor plumbing. They scraped the frost off their bedroom windows in the morning and waited for the kitchen stove to spread its warmth up to their level. Most of the activity in winter was devoted to chopping, splitting and stacking firewood to fuel that kitchen stove, the black iron workhorse that was their primary source of heat and comfort.

Christmas was the only break from the monotony of cold, blistering winds, sleet and driving snow. There was no big build up to Christmas in those days, no countdown to show how many shopping days were left, and very few store windows to press one's nose up against. But there was a feeling, a sense of anticipation that children in Grand Bank shared with children elsewhere. Christmas was special, and it felt like it was created just for them.

School, work and chores continued all the way to Christmas Eve. Then the world as they knew it was magically transformed. She looked forward to the arrival of Santa Claus with a new doll for her and a toy truck for her brother, and, of course, an apple, an orange and a few candies for their stockings.

He claimed not to believe in Santa Claus (we're not really sure about that), but in any case, he looked forward to the slaughtering of a pig every Christmas Eve. Interesting, how boys and girls think so differently!

There were other differences, too. In his house they hung the Christmas tree from the ceiling in the kitchen, probably to save space for the large family. In her house, like most others, the tree stood upright in the parlour. There were a few Christmas decorations – mostly blown balls – but no lights, at least not until hydro came to town years later. But wherever it stood or hung, the Christmas tree was not to be seen by the children until it was ready for them on Christmas morning.

They were packed into their beds early Christmas Eve to snuggle under their ten heavy blankets and await the arrival of Good St. Nick or fresh pork, whichever came first. They scrambled awake at dawn to find their treasures and then go off to church on Christmas morning. After church it was dinnertime, twelve noon on the dot, featuring fresh roast pork as the main course. Maybe that's why he was so excited about killing the pig the night before. Every family in Grand Bank had roast pork for their Christmas meal, and those who were not fortunate enough to have a pig or purchase their own entrée were invited to share in somebody else's Christmas pig.

After a satisfying meal of roast pork, gravy and cabbage, along with whatever vegetables the family could grow themselves, came the Christmas pudding. Sufficiently stuffed, the adults dozed in the kitchen by the warmth of the fire while the children raced outside to show their friends what they got from Santa and to see how well their friends did. It was also time to visit the neighbours' houses, ostensibly to see their Christmas tree which, when pronounced gorgeous, entitled the visitor to a glass of Purity syrup and fruitcake.

On Boxing Day the adults caught up with the children in terms of fun, and every young (and not so young) man and most of the women would begin their rounds of mummering throughout Grand Bank. Men outfitted themselves with women's clothing, often wearing their bloomers on the outside, and women wore men's suits or old fishermen's gear. All of them covered their heads and faces with an assortment of bonnets, hats, scarves or even blankets to hide their sex and identity. Then, seeking entrance for a drink or bite to eat, they would bang on the door of any house with a light on.

"Any mummers 'llowed in?" was the cry heard from doorstep to doorstep, and if you didn't want your cow scared away or your root cellar uprooted, there was little choice but to let a band of roving, fun-loving vagabonds into your kitchen. Sometimes they would sing or dance a little for their victuals, but more often than not they took more sport in insulting the homeowner and making a fool of themselves than in anything else. The drunker they got the more likely you were to be entertained, and you were also more likely to guess their identity, in which case, to the glee of all the other mummers, they had to reveal themselves to their host.

The mummering continued until the last of the twelve days of Christmas and by that time everyone, including the mummers, had probably had enough. Most of the legal alcohol in Grand Bank, and much of the forbidden kind from St. Pierre as well, had been swallowed up in the process. And many a mummer had been dragged home after stumbling into the back of a horse or a cow in the pitch-dark, unlit streets, or after having a short but very drunk nap in a snowbank before being rudely awoken and rescued by their mates.

The other highlight of the Christmas season came on New Year's Eve or "Watch Night" as they called it in Grand Bank. All of the adults and the older children would go to church on New Year's Eve night, and when they returned, the younger children, even the smallest tots, would be roused from their beds so the entire household could enjoy a special meal of soup and pie. It was time to watch the old year go and, by the light of the kerosene lamp in the kitchen, welcome the New Year in.

The dinner was important because it was believed that if you had a full meal on New Year's Eve, you would never go hungry throughout the year.

The memories of those olden Christmas days are

now fading in the twilight but for our two storytellers some are as real as if they happened yesterday. She still has a cherished Christmas doll in a place of honour in their home, and he still recalls a Christmas sleigh that was lovingly made by his father when he was seven or eight. These thoughts and recollections bring a new warmth to the room where they tell their tale.

Christmas today is very different in Grand Bank as it is elsewhere but the spirit of those cold days and warm hearts will live on forever. Times were much simpler then, but they were rich in love and laughter, happiness and joy. And maybe that's the real spirit of Christmas, and as long as we believe in that, then Christmas will never change.

Kasper Barynin

A Windflower Christmas

$\mathcal{I}$t was just days before Christmas, and Sergeant Winston Windflower only had one big problem. That was what to get his girlfriend, Sheila Hillier, for Christmas. Other than that, life was good for the RCMP officer in Grand Bank, Newfoundland. Crime was low, if not non-existent, and spirits were running high as the holiday neared its peak in this little seaside town.

Of course, being the holiday season, the Mountie was concerned about impaired driving. But Windflower and his team had been out on the roads for the past two weekends with the RIDE program. He figured that meant everyone would be on their best behaviour for the next couple of weeks. That was especially true since one town resident had been charged with impaired driving and two others had received suspended licences because they were just over the legal limit of alcohol.

Fortunately, even the weather was cooperating. They hadn't had any snow in Grand Bank for almost two weeks. That was a relief to not only the snow shovellers catching a break after a series of early winter storms but also to the RCMP officers, as they had already worked several overnight shifts because of storms. The best news was that there wasn't even any snow in the short-term forecast.

All of this meant the town could be festive and safe during the holiday season already well underway.

The old Town of Grand Bank went all out to pretty itself up for Christmas. Almost every house had some form of decoration, and Christmas lights were aplenty all over town. Some people went old-fashioned and just had a wreath on their front door and a couple of strings of lights hanging from their eaves. Others decided to splurge on nativity scenes and blow-up Santas, as they held nothing back in their gaudy and joyous celebration of the season.

Old Saint Nick had already made one visit. That was last weekend during the Santa Claus parade led by the antique pumper truck from the volunteer fire department. Local RCMP vehicles were decked out in flashing lights and ribbons as the Mounties collected toys and gifts along the parade route for the Salvation Army. Sheila had rounded up a few extra dollars from local businesses to ensure that even the abandoned buildings near the wharf were gaily festooned with ribbons, bows and the essential Christmas lights in time for the parade. Now, Saint Nick's return engagement on December 25 was eagerly anticipated.

Windflower surprised himself by wishing there would be a bit of snow for Christmas. It just didn't seem right to have brown on the ground and fog in the air at this time of year. Most of the locals agreed as they sat around the Mug-Up Café. Over coffee and tea biscuits, they lamented the lack of snow and collectively prayed for a white Christmas. The RCMP sergeant and his corporal Eddie Tizzard certainly shared this sentiment as they nursed their coffees.

"I know it's happened before, but it doesn't seem right," said Tizzard. "It's not really Christmas without the snow."

Windflower nodded in agreement. "We never had this problem back home," he said, referring to the small Cree community of Pink Lake in Northern Alberta. "By this time of year, we would be frozen down solid with at least a foot of snow on the ground. It made the trees all seem like they were decorated."

"We had a few years like this in Ramea when I was going up, but almost always it would snow on either Christmas Eve or in the morning. I remember one year getting a sled that my dad made me and running out in my pyjamas to try it out," said Tizzard.

Windflower laughed and nodded again. "Here's Sheila," he said when the café door opened and his girlfriend walked in. Sheila made sure to greet each individual in the café personally and with a smile as she made her way over to see Windflower and Tizzard. That's a real politician, thought Windflower.

"Good morning, Sergeant. And good morning, Corporal," said Sheila.

"Morning, Ma'am," said Tizzard just before he put on his hat, nodded and announced to Windflower that he would see him later.

"Good morning to you too, Mrs. Hillier," said Windflower. "I thought you were taking a break from campaigning for the holidays."

"I am," said Sheila. "I'm just being friendly. It doesn't hurt to say hello to folks."

"Or to voters," said Windflower with another laugh.

Sheila laughed, too, and ordered a coffee from the waitress, Marie, when she came by.

"Since I'm not officially running for mayor this week, that'll give us more time to have fun," she said. "There's the Christmas concert tonight and drinks at the Stoodleys first."

"Sounds good," said Windflower. "I'm definitely going back to my kind of running after the holidays. I bet I've put on ten pounds already. Anyway, I gotta get back. See you tonight."

"Okay, Winston, see you later." Sheila took her coffee over to join some of her friends at another table while Windflower waved goodbye before driving the short distance back to work.

Things were slow, slow and very slow at work. But that pace actually suited Windflower these days. It had been an early and busy start to winter. All of the staff at the Grand Bank detachment were looking forward to a break. Tizzard and Windflower would be staying in Grand Bank over the holidays, and they would split the workload, which they both hoped would be minimal.

The other two staff members would be getting a real break this Christmas. Constable Carrie Evanchuk would be going home to Estevan, Saskatchewan. Corporal Harry Frost, who had just arrived as a temporary replacement, had already booked a week in Cuba with his girlfriend. Evanchuk would be leaving late tomorrow, the day before Christmas Eve, and Frost would do the same soon after. That left just enough personnel on duty to keep everything going in Grand Bank until after New Year's.

Even if he had been given time off, Windflower would have had little family to go back to at Christmas. His Uncle Frank and Auntie Marie and a sprinkling of cousins were all that were left in Pink Lake, which was struggling to survive. But it was always like that, he thought. Pink Lake had been impoverished for many years, but to him it was still home, and he always fondly remembered his Christmastimes growing up there.

There were not many gifts, but there was always

a lot of love and food. The whole community saved up for Christmas, and stockpiled food for the community feasting which started December 18 and didn't end until December 21. That was three days of splurging on turkeys and baked hams along with venison roasts, bannock and Windflower's favourite: baked lake trout from the deep, cold water of Northern Alberta. He could also taste the desserts in his mouth every time he thought about them, especially the Saskatoon berry pie with fresh cream that his grandmother made every year at Christmas.

During the twelve days of Christmas every family would have an open house in turn and welcome the community to visit. Windflower remembered trudging from house to house with his parents, and the singing and dancing at every home. While there was some alcohol, there were very few drunks. There was just the spirit of community and the friendship and sharing. It reminded Windflower a little of the mummering tradition in Newfoundland that he was introduced to in his first year in Grand Bank.

He had been sitting in the living room at Sheila's one night between Christmas and New Year's when he heard a loud commotion and a banging on her front door. When he went to the vestibule to answer, he was very surprised to see a band of mummers outside. There were half a dozen people of various shapes and sizes wearing madcap costumes and a bulky, bearded man wearing what looked like a large pair of lady's bloomers over his pants. Their question to Windflower was, "Any mummers 'llowed in?"

He turned to Sheila, now standing beside him, for guidance. She nodded, so he opened the door just a crack. That was all the mummers needed. In a flash, they were inside and quickly arrayed themselves around the living room. They brought a variety of musical instruments with them, including a fiddle and an accordion. The bearded fellow had a large wooden stick with bells and whistles and other things hanging off the side of it. Sheila would tell Windflower later that this was called an "ugly stick," and it was used to keep the beat for the mummers' music.

But that music was not happening, at least at the beginning. In fact, Windflower thought his guests were starting to get upset. One of them openly grumbled about being thirsty and hungry. Luckily, Sheila had gone to the kitchen and came back with a tray of drinks and then with another tray of Christmas cake and cookies. The mummers dug into their food and drinks. Once their appetites were satisfied, they broke into song. A few of them even danced around the living room, and the one with the beard laid down his "ugly stick" long enough to whirl Sheila around a few times. The mummers left shortly afterwards to visit the next house up the road, and Windflower and

Sheila had a good laugh about their entertainment.

Thinking about those good times reminded Windflower how much he liked Christmas. It also jolted him back to the reality that he didn't have Sheila's present yet. He was running out of time. Now was the time to panic. He was still thinking about Sheila's present when he went to pick her up for the Christmas concert. Sheila was as gorgeous as ever and was taking advantage of the milder weather to wear a short strapless dress that highlighted her natural beauty, especially her long, beautiful legs. She wrapped herself in her antique sealskin coat, and they were off to the concert.

He was admiring her as she walked ahead of him, and when she entered the Lions Club building, he thought about the gift again. She had this beautiful coat. Why not get her a pair of matching sealskin boots? But where? Windflower racked his brains through the introductory session by the Men of the Sea choir and again through the Burin Peninsula Irish Dancers. It was only when the children's choir began the last set that it came to him. Ron Quigley was a St. John's boy. He would know where to get the boots.

Windflower thoroughly enjoyed the last of the show, and as soon as he could afterwards, he texted Quigley with his request. Later that evening he was sitting on the couch at Sheila's when his phone buzzed. He picked it up and smiled when he saw the news. Quigley knew of a store in St. John's that stocked sealskin boots for women, and he had sent Windflower the website address.

"What's the good news?" asked Sheila.

"You're not supposed to be asking questions this time of year," said Windflower. "It might spoil your Christmas surprise."

"I'm getting a Christmas surprise?"

"Only if you play your cards right."

"Come on, Sergeant. If there are presents on the line, I have a few more tricks to show you."

Windflower didn't need any more encouragement, and the couple had an absolutely lovely evening together.

The next day Windflower was up early. After his walk with his dog, Lady, he hurried off to work and was on the website that Quigley suggested, looking for the ideal pair of boots for Sheila's present. He found them quickly: "tall, elegant, ladies' one hundred per cent sealskin dress boots." They were black in front and speckled white around the back. They were advertised as "warm, durable and definitely head-turners." That was exactly what Windflower was looking for.

He called the store and asked for a pair in Sheila's size. He had checked her shoe size earlier just before leaving for work. It wasn't much good being a police officer if you couldn't do a little detective work in your personal life, he thought, feeling pretty pleased with his efforts. They had the size, and Windflower told them that someone would be in to pick them up. His next call was to Anna at Froude's Taxi to make that arrangement.

Now, Windflower was set. It was the day before Christmas Eve and he bounced around the office all day. He was even happier than his administrative assistant, Betsy, who had been wearing her lit-up Santa hat for a week now. They had a special lunch at the RCMP detachment that day to celebrate their own Christmas together before the holidays began in earnest, and the good spirits lasted throughout the day and into the evening.

The next morning was Christmas Eve, and Windflower had a special tradition that he always followed on that day. He had learned it from his grandfather who had shared it with Windflower when he was just a small boy. They wandered far out into the forest, following the snowshoe trails, until they came to a clearing. They stood inside a circle of amazing balsam fir trees, each of them rising so high that Windflower thought they touched the sky.

His grandfather did a smudging ceremony inside the balsam grove. He explained that all living things had a spirit. Even these trees had a spirit, an old spirit that lived here long before human beings had arrived. Some called the trees the standing people and believed that they stood sentry to warn all the other creatures when there was danger. Then his grandfather opened his pack and took out a package of nuts and dried berries, along with an apple that he cut into pieces. He and Windflower made small mounds and laid them at intervals around the grove.

They were gifts for their animal friends: the birds, squirrels and rabbits and the larger animals, too. When Windflower asked where the animals were, his grandfather pointed to the trees. "We cannot always see them, but they are always watching us," said his grandfather. Together they prayed silently and then walked home just as silently.

It was a magical and spiritual time for Windflower as he awoke to the animal and natural spirits around him. As a young man he continued this tradition with his grandfather until he died, and still carried it with him wherever he travelled. So today, on Christmas Eve, he and Lady walked in the forest on the nature trail up past the brook in Grand Bank. There was a little snow in parts of the dense forest where trees blocked the sun, and Windflower found a small clearing in the middle of some balsam fir trees, not as tall as the ones back home, but they still reminded him of his early Christmas Eves with his grandfather.

Lady managed to frolic in the thin layer of snow, making sure to taste samples of any varieties of twigs she dug up. While she played, Windflower stood in the middle of the clearing to smudge and say his prayers. He offered his thanks to the trees, the standing people, and to the animals who were watching. He prayed for the spirits of his ancestors, especially those of his grandfather, grandmother and parents, and for the people in his life today, especially Sheila. When he was finished praying, he opened his backpack and took out some dried fruit and berries. He laid them in piles around the area. Lady thought they might be a snack for her and checked them out, but she was just as happy to follow her master as he led the way back to the car.

Windflower went to the RCMP detachment where Betsy was laying out yet another tray of Christmas cookies along with a bottle of Purity syrup. Windflower had never seen or tasted anything like Purity syrup before. It was like liquid sugar that you mixed with water. It came in a variety of flavours from cherry to strawberry to lemon. It was the preferred drink of children and teetotallers, kind of like a Newfoundland Shirley Temple without the cherry on top.

Windflower took a pass on the cookies and syrup, at least for now, and settled for a strong black cup of coffee and a croissant from a package in the lunchroom. He was saving himself for later. He and Sheila would go to church at midnight and afterwards have glazed ham and coleslaw along with freshly made

Parker House rolls.

Christmas Eve at the detachment was a bit of a blur as people kept dropping in to wish him, and the RCMP, Merry Christmas. Just after lunchtime, Tizzard arrived for his shift and joined Windflower in his office to chat. Betsy interrupted the conversation by bringing in a box from St. John's that had been dropped off by Froude's taxi.

"Is that from Santa?" asked Tizzard.

"Christmas secrets," said Windflower, "between Santa and me."

Windflower went out and recruited Betsy to help him wrap his present for Sheila. Wrapping was certainly not his forte. But with his minimal input and Betsy's gift-wrapping acumen, they did a great job. Windflower stayed with Tizzard until about five in the evening and then headed for home. He took Lady for a brisk walk around town and then went over to Sheila's. They had a light snack, and while Sheila finished getting their late-night supper ready, Windflower found It's a Wonderful Life on television.

Soon he and Sheila were happily snuggled together on the couch while George Bailey rediscovered his joy of life with the help of that friendly angel, Clarence. The pair dressed and did a quick walk around town before the midnight service. It was getting a little chillier but was still a very pleasant December evening. They dropped in on the Stoodleys along the way. Together the foursome walked up to the United Church where people from all over Grand Bank were gathering.

An hour later Windflower and Sheila were walking home again, filled with the joyous sounds of Christmas ringing in their ears. Just before they reached their destination, Windflower saw one fat flake and then another fall before them. Soon the air was filled with snow dancing all around. It was a magical sight and warmed their hearts and lifted their spirits even higher.

"Merry Christmas, Sergeant Windflower," said Sheila.

"Merry Christmas, Sheila," he said. "Now let's go open our presents."

David Thompson

Leah Egarhos

The Christmas Surprise

$\mathcal{J}$t was the day before Christmas Eve 1960. I was five and a half years old and filled completely to the brim with the expectations of Christmas. Looking out my kitchen window, I could see large white blobs of snow falling in pieces so large that each snowflake looked like a mouthful. I couldn't wait to get my snowsuit on to go play with my friends, but after I finished my cereal, my mother told me that playtime would have to wait.

Today we were going on a Christmas mission. We had to get a Christmas surprise.

She bundled me up like a mummy from head to toe, and we ventured into the grey, damp morning to head downtown. In those days there were no shopping malls, and we had no car to get to any if there had been. If you wanted or needed anything in St. John's, there was just downtown: a long strip of shops and stores strung out like Christmas lights along the harbour.

My mother promised me that if we walked downtown, we could get the bus home, a false promise designed with the knowledge that my excitement about the Christmas surprise would cause me to forget about it. We needed all our money for the surprise, she told me. That sealed it. I would do anything for Christmas, and she knew it.

So we walked. We set out from our house on Calver Avenue in the neighbourhood called Rabbit Town, named by the gentry in old St. John's who used to hunt in the area before the influx of military bases and inhabitants during the Second World War pushed families past the old boundaries that demarked St. John's.

We trod past the Higher Levels, one of the secondary shopping areas linking the newer neighbourhoods to the traditional multicoloured housing on the hills above the harbour, and down Long's Hill.

Long's Hill reminded me of a giant ski jump. It had to be designed with snow sliders and tobogganers in mind because its slope was steep, elegant and, well, long. In the winter it was studiously avoided by all drivers without steel chains on their tires, and it seemed no amount of salt or gravel made it less treacherous.

It wasn't the steepest hill in St. John's though. That honour probably belonged to Barters Hill which was an almost perfect incline straight downwards. It was the site of a horrific accident years later when an oil truck lost its brakes and crashed through the Sears store window at the bottom.

Long's Hill was great to go down. My mother tried to hold me, but I was determined to slide down most of the way on my boots and even on my bum as I faked an accident to get a better ride. I was prepared to listen to her cackle for my brief moments of downhill joy. Sooner than I hoped, we reached the bottom, and after a quick meander through a few alleys, we reached our destination.

Downtown held no attraction for me during the year and usually meant "the trip" to get my new school clothes or, even worse, just to tag along behind my mother or my sisters as they shopped. I can never remember my father being there for the shopping though. Maybe he got an exemption, but perhaps it was because the shops were only open then during the same hours that he worked.

Downtown at Christmastime was a wide-eyed child's delight. I don't remember everything, but the sounds and smells will linger forever.

Every store, it seemed, had a loudspeaker outside that blared Christmas music to passersby. I still remember Silver Bells as my favourite. Every shop, large and small, had a decorated window with toys and their latest fashions on display. I remember being just shuffled along from each window leaving my nose print along with hundreds of others as my mark to the power of their advertising. Toy buying would have to wait until another day – or decade.

St. John's back then had none of the modern retail giants that we see today but instead featured a series of unique family-owned enterprises. Ayre's department store was founded by one of the city's richest families and sought to serve the lower middle class by fulfilling the material aspirations of most St. John's residents. Other choices included The London, New York and Paris, a store that had somewhat higher-end selections on its upper floors and, for the less well off, a bargain basement in the bowels of the building across from the courthouse. It also had one of those fabulous in-store money delivery systems where payments were sent up a metal tube to the cashier, and change and a receipt came back down to the clerk. I always hoped that my mother would buy something there just so that I could watch this miracle system at work.

But it was the Arcade that was the most interesting store in St. John's, especially at Christmastime. The all-bargain all-the-time emporium had customers ranging from the Baymen (anyone from outside St. John's), who were in town for their yearly Christmas adventure, to the remnants of the Portuguese fishing fleet marooned in St. John's for the holidays. The smell of wet mittens mixed with tobacco and salt fish was actually not as bad as it sounds. To a child it felt exotic and exciting, like the fear of the unknown.

Mom would grip me tightly as we browsed through the trinkets, hand-knitted socks and Christmas kitsch that made up the Arcade inventory. That was just in case some Portuguese sailor tried to kidnap me and spirit me away to be a cabin boy on their ocean travels. Actually, I thought that sounded exciting. I gazed at the browner men as they scooped up plastic Virgin Marys and glow-in-the-dark Jesus dolls and hoped they would see me as a willing recruit. But they would carefully avoid me with gestures I would come to realize later were based on fears of survival as aliens in a foreign and sometimes unfriendly stopover.

I can't say I remember much of the shopping, but when it finally came time for lunch, I noticed that my mother's arms were laden with bags, parcels and one large box. She bundled them carefully into a small booth at my favourite restaurant, the Sweet Shop.

You could smell the Sweet Shop long before it came into viewing range. It smelled like strawberry shortcake, which of course was one of its specialties along with lemon meringue pie. It also had the best French fries anywhere.

I had my regular lunch, a small plate of French fries drenched in salt and malt vinegar. I wanted the large plate and promised I could eat them all but always settled for the smaller version and a full stomach.

It seemed to me like everyone knew each other in St. John's, or maybe they just pretended to. In any case, there was a steady bantering and cheery greetings of "Merry Christmas!" exchanged throughout our all-too-brief sojourn at the Sweet Shop.

There was one more stop to make, and then we would head home. It was our annual visit to the Mount Cashel Raffle. It was easy to find. You just followed the sound of the ringing bells.

Outside on the sidewalk stood one of the boys from Mount Cashel, the oldest and only boys' orphanage in St. John's, glumly ringing a time-worn cow bell. I couldn't understand why he seemed unhappy. Though I know better now, back then I would have gladly taken his place of honour guarding such a welcome event.

In the window of the Raffle storefront, there was a nativity scene and live turkeys gobbling around. That, for a nearly six-year-old boy, was the main attraction. Yanked once again by my too-often-wrung neck, I was plunged into the chaos of the Raffle.

Crowds of people gathered around with ticket stubs protruding from an assortment of hand wear, from fancy, leather gloves to threadbare, hand-knit fishermen's mitts. All social and economic sphere mingled at the Raffle. They were all Catholic, of course, but since I didn't know anyone who wasn't, it seemed like the whole world was at the Raffle.

We didn't win a box of Pot of Gold chocolates or a turkey to go, but my mother felt that it was a good way to support a solid Catholic institution, as Mount Cashel was thought to be back then.

The Raffle continued on in a similar form for many years to come until a sexual abuse scandal forced many of the Christian Brothers who ran the place into jail or exile. But when I was a kid, those were good times. At least people pretended that to be the case, and for a young boy living in town, I was just happy to be really close to a live turkey.

Now it was time for the long trudge home. Having forgotten about my mother's promise to take the bus back, we started to retrace our steps up the hill to the Higher Levels.

We were about half way up Long's Hill when I remembered the promised deal, and instead of trying to negotiate with my mother, which I knew was useless, I just lay down in the snow and refused to move any further.

My mother didn't react the way I had hoped, which would've been to feel sorry for me and immediately apologize for breaking her promise to her only son. Instead, she bent over and whispered in my ear, "Don't you want to see the Christmas surprise?" A few fake tears later (I couldn't let her know that it was all an act), I was begging her to tell me what the surprise was. Despite my pleadings and prayers, all she would say was, "Wait 'til we get home."

So what was keeping her then? I don't remember walking home the rest of the way. I don't know if my feet even touched the ground. Mercifully, it wasn't too long, and after we had taken off our coats and boots and mittens and scarves, she took out the large box that I suddenly remembered from the Sweet Shop.

My eyes glowed as she removed the cardboard and then the plastic wrapping. What was it?

It looked like a small plastic blue suitcase, but when she opened it up, it was an electric record player. From inside another bag she pulled out four small, black 78 RPM records, plugged the record player in, and wonder of all wonders it began to sing. The first record was the Witch Doctor with a crazy chorus that went "ooo eee, ooh ah ah ting tang, walla walla, bing bang." I loved it!

The next one was Running Bear by Johnny Preston that told the story of a young brave who loved an Indian girl but wasn't allowed by their families to be with her and drowned while trying to swim across the river to meet her. It was sad but absolutely fascinating. There were others like El Paso by Marty Robbins and Tom Dooley by the Kingston Trio, and my favourite Christmas song, Silver Bells.

I demanded and got my mother to play them over and over again. This was our Christmas surprise, a record player. I was thrilled. But in order for it to remain a surprise for my father and especially my three older sisters, I was sworn to secrecy by my mother at pain of not getting anything from Santa if I let out one peep about it to anybody.

That was threat enough.

Besides, for the first time in my life I knew a

surprise before anybody else. Having three older sisters meant that I was always the last to know anything, if they decided to tell me at all. I finally had something on them. The Christmas surprise was safe with me.

My mother wasn't so sure, and I don't think that she ever left me out of her eyesight or earshot for the rest of the day, especially after my sisters got home from school shortly afterwards. I wanted to tell them about the Christmas surprise, but I certainly wasn't going to risk my chances with Santa by giving them the inside scoop.

The day turned to dusk early and then into darkness. That evening my father took the whole family on the bus to travel all over the city to see the Christmas lights. That was a magical evening as the light snow turned every festive display into a miniature vision of what I assumed the North Pole was like. Exhausted from my shopping excursion and the tour of the city, I fell into that comfortable black hole that envelops small children at Christmastime.

When I awoke, it was Christmas Eve, the big day. Mom was already up and had the Christmas turkey defrosting in a pan under the kitchen table. She smiled and winked at me, her co-conspirator, and I winked back, a sign that the secret was still safe with me. The rest of the day was pretty much a blur of visitors and comings and goings of the rest of my family, who as usual were happy to ignore me.

Only my mother kept a watchful eye over me as if she fully expected me at any point to blurt out the good news from under the table where Tom, our Christmas turkey, and I were happily singing all the songs that were on our new playlist.

Soon enough it was time for bed, at least for me, and I was grateful that the wait was just about over. After a few minutes torn between wondering if I would ever fall asleep and trying to listen for Santa's arrival, I fell into the best of all sleeps, the Christmas sleep.

I awoke with a start. It was light and it was Christmas morning.

As usual, I was the first one out of the bedrooms to confirm that Santa had indeed arrived. I was pretty sure the pair of new used skates, the new hockey stick and the puck were all for me. And there, too, was the Christmas surprise in its camouflaged blue suitcase.

"He came, he came, Santa came," I screamed as the sound of weary bones trickled out from my parent's bedroom. My sisters trudged out, too, sleepy but excited.

"There's a Christmas surprise for the whole family," I yelled. "And I know what it is?" My mother gave me a half-frown, but I had kept my end of the bargain. It was Christmas morning and all bets were off.

My mother took the blue suitcase up from underneath the Christmas tree and set it up on the kitchen table. I looked underneath, but Tom had already been dressed and stuffed for dinner. My few disconsolate moments over his demise were quickly shattered by the sounds of glee from my three older siblings.

They gushed and gooed and aahed and oohed. When it started to sing, they laughed and sang along.

To them it was the best Christmas ever, but for me it was all about being a collaborator in the great Christmas surprise. The following year, we got another surprise – my baby brother – and things were never as special or as unique between my mother and me again. My preferred status as "the baby" of the family was usurped by this interloper, and I now had to suffer the horrors of being a middle child and of going to school, too. Yes, there were other Christmases and even other Christmas surprises, but my mother shared them early only with my younger brother, who became her new shopping companion while my sisters and I were in school.

I never felt as good again about Christmas until I had my own children many years later. Then I realized that it doesn't really matter what you get for Christmas or even what you give. As long as you are grateful to the moment of Christmas and welcoming to its spirit of love, there will always be another Christmas surprise. You just don't know what it will be yet. Close your eyes and imagine it. And maybe, just maybe, it will be under your tree on Christmas morning.

Briana Nykilchyk

Christmas on the Corner

The anticipation had been feverishly building for weeks, but we just went about our daily routines, hoping that busyness would make the time go faster. We'd get up in the dark, bundle ourselves off to school, often wading through chest-high drifts of snow to get to our classroom. Inside the school, there was a tangled mess of wet boots whose odour mingled with the sharp aroma of fifty pairs of woollen mitts on radiators, their owners hoping they would be dry enough for snowball making on the way home.

School was a blur of activity as the Christian Brothers at St. Pat's tried to dampen the enthusiasm of hundreds of boys who had nothing on their minds but Christmas. The Brothers had little chance of success, but that didn't seem to stop them from singling out one boy after another for particular attention, hoping that the others would learn from the experience of those they made to suffer. It did little but momentarily dull the quiet roar that lived inside each of us, only to soon erupt again, and another prisoner would head to the gallows.

Finally, school would be over for the day and it would be our time. We laughed, fought and danced our way home. There'd be just enough time for a quick drink and snack, and then it was on to the eternal street hockey game. We played street hockey every day after school from the first snowfall, usually sometime in October, to the last snow on the ground, often well into April.

We used a tennis ball because those fancy orange hockey balls froze quickly in the cool winter air, and when you got hit with a slapshot, it felt like getting shot by a cannonball. Besides, none of us had hockey pads. A few had hockey gloves, but most just bundled their sticks into the maw of their mitts, which after an hour or two were each ten pounds heavier from the cold outside and the sweat inside. We didn't have any hockey nets either. That would come much later. Instead we used lumps of snow as posts, and this created an endless debate about whether a shot was a goal or "over the post." When it came to our sticks, most of us had cheap – really cheap – wooden ones that we got at a hardware store in the neighbourhood. If your stick got broken, you just played on with the stump.

But boy was it fun! It didn't matter if there were just two players, although there were usually enough to make up teams of four or five. We set up in the middle of the road, and it was game on. We moved out of the way of cars, but not everybody had a car, and there was little traffic on our street. Our biggest worry was the cops. Two or three of our neighbours didn't like the idea of us taking over the street, so every day we played, they called the police to get us off the road. It was illegal to play hockey on the street, but I'm not even sure there was a penalty for doing so.

It was a great adventure when someone spied a cop car coming. "Cops!" they would yell, and we would all scatter over the snowbanks and into the backyards near the action. Breathless, we would lay low until the police had passed. They never got out of the car, but we still ran as if we were wanted for murder. I think the cops probably had a good laugh at the sight of all these little hoodlums running for their lives. As soon as we thought the coast was clear, we would regroup at our hangout, the Corner.

St. John's at that time was a series of small enclaves, each bounded by the street on which you lived. None of these streets were very long, but sometimes your gang only extended for part of the street. You could know someone in another section, but it was unlikely they could be your friend, and they certainly couldn't hang around with you. Calver Avenue was an east-west street of about eighty homes. But it had at least four distinct sections. The headquarters of our gang was Morecombe's Corner, designated by the grocery store at the corner of Calver Avenue and Mayor Avenue.

Just about every corner in St. John's had its own corner store, mostly mom and pop operations that sold the basics: dry goods, soft drinks, potato chips, a meagre selection of prepared meats and maybe a few vegetables like potatoes, turnip and carrots. They would also carry cigarettes and tobacco, soap and detergent, and if you brought a note from your mother, you could get a package of sanitary napkins. All of us hated getting that note, and we would sneak into the store and hope nobody noticed what we were getting. We didn't know what they were, but there were always some older boys hanging around who would tease you mercilessly if they found you with them.

We didn't have much money, nobody did, but every so often we would beg a few cents from our moms to get a snack and drink at the store. We didn't need much money. A Coke was a dime, a bag of chips five cents, and later when we started smoking you got two cigarettes for a nickel. The best times were after a snowstorm when we would trudge around the neighbourhood offering to "clear people's paths" for them. When we got lucky and one of the shut-ins engaged us, half a dozen of us would furiously shovel our way to enough money for all of us to head to Morecombe's for a Coke and maybe a raisin square.

Once it got dark, it was time to go home for supper, homework, a little TV and then off to bed, exhausted but excited since Christmas was only two days away and there was just one more day of school before Christmas. I don't think my feet touched the ground on the way to school the next morning, and my head was higher than the drifting snow that by now had reached near the tops of telephone poles in places. All the talk was about what we were getting for Christmas.

I didn't have any great expectations because I knew that we couldn't afford most of the things that were advertised on TV, but some of my friends had already sneaked into their parents' bedrooms and seen the stacks of boxes that they hoped were for them. My dream was for a pair of real hockey gloves like the NHL players had, preferably in Chicago Blackhawk colours, but as I had told my mother many times, anything but the dreaded blue and white of the Maple Leafs would be fine.

The day at school passed quickly, and we hurried home for one last game of hockey before Christmas Eve. At home, I reminded my mother of my special Christmas request. She shooed me away with a warning about the perils of bad behaviour just before Christmas and of getting my clothes soaked playing street hockey, a warning that was impossible to heed. The game went faster than the school day, and before I knew, it was time for bed and the long deep sleep of a hopeful child.

As usual, that Christmas Eve was a hubbub of activity with relatives dropping in and the happy sounds of a few alcoholic drinks being passed around. Anyone who came to our house on Christmas Eve was guaranteed one drink – and one drink only. My mother would get the bottle of whisky out of its secret cupboard and quickly return it to its hiding place as soon as the drink was delivered.

We played hockey all day that day, got chased by the police twice and managed to hitch a ride on the back bumper of an oil truck going down the steep incline of Avalon Street near my house. "Getting a cling" was a great adventure full of potential danger and extreme excitement. Part of the thrill was the stories we had been told of youngsters sliding beneath the wheels and perishing under enormous weight and power. We didn't really believe the stories, but if they were true, something like that couldn't happen to us because we were invincible.

We said goodbye and wished each other much success in the Santa department. Then it was home to wring out our dripping clothes and have one last meal before Christmas. We didn't have anything fancy, sausages and potatoes I think, but it was still one of the greatest meals of the year. Then it was time to watch Don Jamieson, who later served in Prime Minister Pierre Trudeau's cabinet, celebrate Christmas on TV with his family. All of us huddled together to watch and listen as Don read *'Twas the Night Before Christmas*, and even though I protested, it was time for bed.

I tried my best to fall asleep but couldn't, so I listened for any signs of Santa Claus. I didn't hear any reindeer on the roof, but I did hear a lot of rustling going on out in the living room. Finally, and thankfully, I drifted off to sleep. When I awoke, it was Christmas morning, and as usual I was the first one under the tree. My eyes grew wide as I saw my hockey gloves, not completely new but looking just as real as the ones that my heroes wore. They weren't Blackhawk gloves, but they were those of the Montreal Canadiens, my dad's team. I could live with that. At least they weren't blue. Soon I had woken the rest of my family, and they all stumbled out to see what Christmas had brought them. I have no idea what anyone else got. I was already wearing my gloves and showing off my shooting style with my new fifty-cent hockey stick.

Then it was time for our stockings, and while we didn't get a lot, I really appreciated what we did get. We always got a big red Christmas apple that I ate first, an orange that could wait and a handful of grapes that we as children only ever saw at Christmas. There were a few little toys, a new pair of socks and mitts, and at the very bottom of the stocking, a glorious Cracker Jack box.

That Christmas, after I ate my apple, I pulled open

my Cracker Jack box and dug to the bottom to find my toy, and as I was figuring out how to put together the miniature boat, I savoured each sweet morsel of sticky caramel-coated peanuts and popcorn. At this point, my mother and older sisters were pushing me to get ready for Mass, and for some reason they wouldn't let me wear my new hockey gloves to church.

After Mass we came home and had a delicious turkey dinner and then settled in to watch the Christmas programs on TV. They included the old version of A Christmas Carol, a few cartoons like Rudolph and the story of Heidi. The little lost girl in the Swiss Alps didn't interest me at all. I would've preferred Swiss Family Robinson, but my sisters would never have allowed that. Besides, the only two viewing options at that time on Christmas were the message from the Queen and Heidi. Heidi would be just fine.

Anyway, I would've much rather been able to just go out and play hockey with my friends. But Christmas was one of the only two days that hockey was off limits, the other being Good Friday. Today was supposed to be a family day, but after the gifts were opened and dinner eaten, I just wanted the day to be over so I could be back out on the Corner with my buddies.

Then we could see what everyone got and plan how we were going to get even better stuff next year at Christmas on the Corner.

Isabella Valentino

Kaya Johnson

Can Windflower Save Christmas?

*I*t's three days to Christmas, and the little Town of Grand Bank, Newfoundland, is ready. The decorations have been up for weeks, and the recent Santa Claus parade was a great success. One of the highlights was the appearance of Santa himself. In dramatic fashion, he came down out of the sky in the RCMP helicopter and showered all the little kiddies and their parents with an assortment of candies and chocolates.

Sgt. Winston Windflower thought that had been a particularly nice surprise, even if he had arranged it with his friend Corporal Ted Reid, who had just happened to be in the vicinity with his helicopter, on the day of the parade.

Now that Christmas was so close, the excitement was building. So was the anxiety amongst the parents in the town.

The weather had been mild so far this winter. That was normally a good thing, but it came with more than a few difficulties. First, a series of rainstorms had damaged some of the roads and bridges, including parts of the highway outside Grand Bank. Then it had started snowing days ago, and it had never seemed to stop. It was beautiful to look at, but it was starting to accumulate and made driving, and even walking, treacherous.

Finally, the snow was tapering off but being replaced by a fog so thick that it felt like it might just smother the small town. In a few days, the fog would melt the snow from the inside out, but for today, Grand Bank was snowbound and fogbound too.

Just when he thought things couldn't get any worse, they did. Windflower got a call from the Highways Department that the bridge outside Grand Beach, a few miles from Grand Bank on the road to Marystown and Swift Current, had collapsed under the weight of the snow. No one was hurt, but it did mean no one could drive in or out of Grand Bank. That was unlikely to change, at least until after the holidays.

Might as well break the bad news now, thought Windflower. He put on his boots, grabbed his hat and coat and went to the front of the Grand Bank RCMP Detachment. There, Betsy Molloy, the long-time administrative mastermind behind the operation, was talking on the phone. She put her headset down when she saw Windflower approach. "The road's out," she said before Windflower could say anything. Windflower smiled. Obviously, the chatter line was more effective than the official one. "I'm going to see the mayor," he told her.

He decided to walk the short distance to the town office. It was a short distance to everywhere in Grand Bank. He didn't mind the fog but hoped it wouldn't last too long. If it did, they wouldn't have any snow left for Christmas. He was still pondering that thought when he walked into the office and almost bumped into Sheila, Mayor Sheila Hillier, his wife and soon-to-be mother of their child.

"Oops," said Windflower as he caught Sheila in his arms. "Are you okay?"

"I will be when you let me out of this Vulcan death grip," she said with a laugh. "Shouldn't you be out trying to get our highway repaired? The road's out, you know."

"That's what I came to see you about," said Windflower, a touch of exasperation creeping into his voice as he discovered, once again, that he was the last to get important news in this little community. "They're saying that it'll be at least a week this time," he added.

"What about Christmas?" asked Sheila. "I've already had parents in here wondering when their packages are going to arrive. Many of them ordered Christmas presents for their children, and now they won't get here in time. I even ordered something for you."

"For me? What is it?"

When he saw the grimace on Sheila's face, Windflower decided he had better quickly change the subject. "I was thinking," (and this time it was real fast thinking since he had just come up with it) "that maybe I could get Ted Reid to do a special run in the helicopter."

"That might work, but not with the weather like this," said Sheila. "If the fog doesn't lift, we might have to postpone Christmas."

"We can't do that," said Windflower. "One year in Pink Lake when I was small, we got socked-in by weather for a week just before Christmas. Nobody could get in or out. We had our families but no presents for Christmas. We thought Santa had forgotten about us. I don't want any other child to go through that."

"What are you going to do?"

"I don't know yet, but if there's any way possible, we have to save Christmas."

Sheila gave her man a hug, and he squeezed her back. He was walking back to the office when he decided to make a short detour. He went back home and picked up Lady, his four-year-old collie. She was very happy to join him as they wandered down over the beach and up the hill toward the Grand Bank Cape.

The snow was deep but soft, and it made the going slow. By the time the pair got to the first rise on the pathway, they were both panting. Lady had several large mouthfuls of snow while Windflower sat on a large rock to think. He couldn't see much, but like always when he came up here, his thinking became clearer and clearer. He didn't come up with any answers; he wasn't that good. But he knew who to ask. His friend Herb Stoodley was just the person to talk to when you had a problem. And if he didn't have an answer, you could always get a piece of chocolate peanut butter cheesecake at the café.

Windflower strolled down the hill with Lady at his heels, dropped the dog at home and walked to Mug-Up Café to see if Herb was available for a chat. After getting them both a coffee and Windflower his cheesecake, they settled into a corner of the warm restaurant for their talk. Herb listened, nodded and sympathized while Windflower described the plight.

"It would be sad not to have the presents," Herb said when Windflower finished. "But when we were small, there wasn't very much, and we made do with what we had – maybe a homemade sled or doll for the girls, a few Christmas candies and an apple from the barrel that Uncle Bob Riggs used to bring over on his horse and carriage from Marystown. We still had a great Christmas."

"That's it!" exclaimed Windflower.

"What's it?" asked Herb Stoodley in surprise.

"We don't have a horse and carriage. But we do have horsepower in our snowmobiles and a couple of trailers. I can drive over to Marystown on a snowmobile and bring them back. I gotta run. I gotta tell Sheila."

Minutes later Windflower was in Sheila's office again and breathlessly told her his plan.

"That's great," she said. "I'll call a meeting of the parents and see if we can make a list of what they have over in Marystown. But we'll need someone over there to pick it all up and package it for us."

"I'll get on the phone to Ron and see if his guys can help," said Windflower, referring to his long-time friend Inspector Quigley. "I'll see you soon."

Windflower went back to his office where Betsy smiled at him on his way in. "I'm so proud of you," she said. "You're going to save Christmas."

Windflower thought of asking how she knew what was going on, but gave up and just nodded. "Can you get Inspector Quigley on the line?"

"Yes, Sir," said Betsy.

The phone in his office was blinking when he got there. "Inspector Quigley on line one," said Betsy over the intercom.

"Ron, how are you?" asked Windflower.

"I am well," said the inspector. "I hear you are trying to save Christmas."

"Why does everybody know stuff around here, and even over there, before I do?"

"It may be the spirits of the season," Quigley laughed. "How can I help Sergeant Christmas?"

"Very funny," said Windflower, and he ran through his plan with Quigley. "As long as the weather stays the way it is, I should be okay."

"That might be a bit of a problem. The forecast is for a Christmas blast from the north. At least twenty-five centimetres. That could be fifty by the time it hits around here. It's supposed to start soon and last about twenty-four hours."

Windflower refused to be disheartened, although he knew that much snow would make conditions ever more treacherous for man, beast or even snow machine. "I should still be okay on the snowmobile," he said.

"Well, we'll do our best to do what we can from our end here in Marystown. I'll get some of my folks on it right away. They'll be happy to help out."

"That would be great. Thanks, Ron. And Frost is visiting with friends near Marystown. I'll get him to contact you so you can put him to work, too. He might be crusty on the outside but he's just a real softy on the inside. He'll love it."

The rest of the day flew by and so did the next day. Sheila was busy coordinating the lists of presents from the parents, and Windflower had volunteered

Betsy to work with Marystown to pick the gifts up and get them all together. Later in the day, he placed a call to Corporal Harry Frost, who sounded exhausted but excited at the same time.

"I think we got them all, or we'll pick up the last ones in the morning," said Frost. "Just want to warn you that there's at least two loads, but we should be able to get it all done."

"That's great, Corporal," said Windflower. "But we'll have to see how it goes. If it's too dangerous, maybe neither or us will make it back home, and we'll have to hunker down in Marysville for Christmas."

"It'll be fine, like an adventure. And the kids, I can't stand thinking of them not having presents for Christmas."

Windflower laughed. "Yes, Harry. I know what you mean. But let's cross those bridges when we come to them, okay? And I think everything will work out."

He was still smiling about his conversation with one of Newfoundland's longest-serving Mounties when he told Sheila about it later as they were getting ready for bed. She didn't think there was anything to smile about, though. "You have to promise me that you'll turn back if it's not safe, okay?" She held him and wouldn't let him go until he promised.

He promised and hugged her back until she fell asleep in his arms. Then he got up to take one more look outside. The good news was that the fog had miraculously dissipated. The bad news was that many fat, fast and furious snowflakes were starting to fall from the sky. Plus, the wind was picking up. Not good signs at all.

In the morning, Windflower's worst fears were realized. While the fog was long gone, a wall of blinding, driving snow now made it impossible to see across the road. There was a thick blanket of snow on the ground and much more coming down by the hour.

Windflower had a quick breakfast with Sheila and got to the office early. Betsy gave him an update on the progress of the package collection in Marystown. Everything would be ready just after lunchtime.

The other RCMP officers had been working to get the best of the two RCMP snowmobiles ready for Windflower. It was a sturdy machine, a bit of a beast and, while slower than the speed demons of today, quite reliable and capable of towing almost anything behind it. Windflower packed his emergency supplies and extra gas can in a large trailer and got ready for the trip.

Just before noon he started up the snowmobile and drove by the town office to say goodbye to Sheila. Bundled up in his snow gear and with his fur Mountie hat on, he looked a little like an explorer heading out for new territory. He was turning onto the highway to Marystown when he saw the snowplow flashing its lights behind him. It was Evan Shortall, the local plow operator. He'd come to give Windflower an escort to the end of town.

At the Grand Beach turnoff Shortall flashed his snowplow lights and allowed Windflower to pass by. Soon it was only Windflower with the machine roaring in his ears and the wind and snow biting into any part of his body that was exposed. It was only about an hour's drive by car to Marystown, under normal driving conditions. But these were hardly normal conditions. Windflower followed the road all along the way until he came to the place where it had been washed out.

He swerved off the road and followed the ditch alongside the collapsed bridge. That's when he saw the exposed wires hanging down from the hydro pole. Actually, he didn't see them at first; he heard the buzzing and was able to move back from the danger zone before his machine came into contact with the live wires. He called back in to report the additional damage and continued on.

He passed a couple of more mini-washouts and each time dipped into the ditch and went around the obstacle. Despite the lack of visibility, he was making good time and was starting to think this would be much easier than planned. That's when he hit the next ditch. He had swooped around the semi-collapsed bridge somewhere past the last Garnish turnoff when he felt the ground, and his machine, sink beneath him. "Uh-oh," he said out loud. Uh-oh was right. He managed to get off the snowmobile just as it was sinking up to its handlebars in mud and muck. There must have been a bit of water underneath in that spot and the snow had covered it up. Windflower grabbed his knapsack out of the trailer as it too dipped down to its cover. Inside was an industrial flashlight, a small axe, some matches, flares, water and a couple of emergency meal kits. He pulled his phone out of his pocket and tried to call back into Grand Bank. No service. "Shoot," he muttered to himself.

There were few options open to him, so he picked up his pack and went back on the highway. He figured he was about halfway between Grand Bank and Marystown and maybe fifteen klicks back to Garnish. There was almost no chance of anyone being on the highway back there, so he might as well start off for Marystown. There was still plenty of light, and he hoped that he could at least make it close to Winterland before dusk.

Even though he had the capacity to make a fire, he certainly didn't relish a night in the Newfoundland woods. So he started walking along as fast as he could. Slogging might be a better word for it. The snow was thick and deep, and the wind in his face was bitter and biting, but at least the effort was keeping him warm. He walked for about an hour, and while it felt like four, he knew that he was making little progress toward his goal. He was starting to get discouraged when he thought he saw a light up ahead on the highway. I hope this isn't some kind of snow mirage, he thought.

He stopped and waited to see if the light got closer. He heard that was one way to tell a mirage from the real thing. This was the real thing. It was a vehicle and it was loud. When it got closer, he could see it was a large black SUV, an RCMP SUV. It came right up to him, and a familiar face became visible through the haze of the snow. It was Harry Frost.

"Hey, Sarge, are you okay?" shouted Frost over the wind and the noise from the vehicle.

Windflower nodded and let Frost grab his knapsack while he jumped into the back of the SUV. In the driver's seat was Inspector Ron Quigley.

"We figured that something must have happened. Grand Bank called over an hour ago to say that they tried to reach you but had lost contact," said Quigley.

"Betsy," murmured a shivering Windflower, now starting to feel the chill as he thawed out.

"Yeah, she called me," said Frost. "Here's a cup of coffee to warm you up." He passed Windflower a thermos cup of coffee.

Windflower sipped it slowly even though he wanted to slurp the whole cup down as fast as he could to warm up. "I hit a ditch, and the machine just sunk in," he said after a few sips of hot coffee thawed out his lips.

"No worries, we'll get it when the storm clears," said Quigley. "We'll get you back to Marystown and warmed up for the night."

"I've got to go back," said Windflower. "We can't let the children miss Christmas."

Quigley laughed. "Okay, okay. Just warm up and relax. Frost and I are going to Grand Bank with you, so you should be safe this time."

"Turns out we need three trailers," said Frost. "You won't believe how much stuff we have."

It was still snowing heavily when they reached the outskirts of Marystown. If it was possible, the wind had picked up even more. When they came to the Creston North exit, Windflower saw the barriers and the flashing signal lights indicating that the road was closed to regular traffic. There were also two RCMP cars parked next to the barricades, and when they saw the SUV, they turned on their lights and sirens and followed Windflower.

"What's this about?" asked Windflower, now comfortable enough to take off his hat and mitts.

"You're famous, Boss," said Frost. "They're calling you Sergeant Christmas."

"Who's calling me that?" asked Windflower.

"Everyone," said Quigley. As they were driving

to the RCMP detachment in Marystown, the few remaining drivers on the roads all flashed their lights at Windflower and his entourage.

"One of the local radio stations found out about you coming over," said Quigley. "Now everybody's talking about it. People have been dropping off gifts and toys for Grand Bank ever since. You're famous b'y."

When they got to the RCMP detachment, the parking lot was full and people were coming in and out of the building like ants in an anthill. When they saw the SUV pull up, people rushed out of the offices, and when Windflower got out of the SUV, he was mobbed by well-wishers. There was even a reporter from the Southern Gazette trying to get a comment from him.

"We'll have Sgt. Windflower available for comments in a few minutes," Quigley said, grabbing Windflower by the arm and moving him quickly into his office.

"What's all this?" asked Windflower, his voice finally restored.

"People are looking for a good news story. And you're it," said Quigley. "I might have pushed it along a little bit. It's good community relations. But I think it was worth it. Come on out back."

Windflower followed Quigley and Frost out to the garage. He couldn't believe his eyes. There were stacks and stacks of parcels and presents and what looked like platters of cooked turkey and a whole mini-section of baking tins that he was sure contained homemade cakes and cookies.

"There's enough for an army here," he finally said in amazement.

"We're going to split it between you and the women's shelter and the Sally Ann in Marystown," said Quigley

Windflower laughed. "Wow. This is amazing."

"The power of good in the world," said Quigley. "Now, if you're okay, we'll meet the reporter and get that out of the way. Then we'll take a break for a while, and when you're ready, we should get back to it. The snow is still coming down out there."

A couple of hours later, all three men and their sleds were loaded with their parcels and goodies and ready to head over to Grand Bank. They got an escort of RCMP vehicles to the edge of town, and all along the way people came out of shops and their homes to wave to the Mountie parade that was passing through.

Windflower waved shyly to the people as they passed. He wasn't much for drawing attention to himself. But he had to smile all the same. This was pretty cool, he thought. "Sergeant Christmas, I like the sound of that," he said to himself as their snowmobile motorcade slipped out of Marystown and back on to the highway.

It was dark and still heavily snowing as the

snowmobile cavalcade left the lights of Marystown for the dark highway. The machines were a bit slower than optimum because they were pulling heavy loads, but the trio of Mounties still made good time on their journey. Then, just before they came to the place where Windflower had his disaster earlier, the wind started to slow and so too did the snow. It was like the remaining wind blew all of the clouds out of the sky, and one by one the stars magically appeared.

Soon the moon came out, too, and with the reflection from the snow, it was almost like daytime. The three men stopped and shut off their engines. They stood quietly for a minute, transfixed by the scene in front of them. No one spoke as they shared what Windflower knew was a spiritual moment together. He gave thanks for his friends and allies and silently said a short prayer of gratitude for all the gifts that he had already received.

Half an hour later they came over the rise outside of Grand Beach and could see the twinkling lights of Grand Bank in the near distance. As they got closer to the little town that Windflower now called home, they were met by another escort. This time it was Evan Shortall with his snowplow all lit up and decorated with Christmas lights and a shining star on top of his cab. He was joined by local Mounties in two cruisers with lights flashing, leading Windflower and his snowmobile crew into town.

At the edge of town some people had gathered on their own snowmobiles and followed the RCMP cruisers into Grand Bank. By the time the Mounties got to the centre of town, there were dozens of snow machines behind them. At the Lions Club, another hundred or so men, women and children were waiting, and everyone cheered when the snowmobiles with the presents arrived. Santa Claus, who bore a remarkable resemblance to Herb Stoodley, greeted Windflower, Frost and Quigley and gave them each a Santa hat to wear.

Sheila and some of the women unloaded the food first and laid it out on tables which were already groaning with sweets, candies and cakes. The men helped sort out the presents, and once everyone was in place, Santa started calling up the children one by one and giving them their presents. Sheila came over to the three Mounties and gave them each a mug of hot spiced rum and a hug. She gave Windflower a special embrace, and they held each other tightly as the happy scene unfolded in front of them.

There were squeals of delight all around as the children opened gifts and started playing with their dolls and other toys right in the middle of the floor. The adults watched with an equal joy and sipped and nibbled their way through the next few totally enjoyable hours. As they left for the night, each of the adults came to shake Windflower's hand to thank him for making this Christmas so special.

Approaching Windflower and holding his hand out, Frost said, "You're a good man, Sergeant. I don't think I've ever said that to anyone before, but I want you to know how I feel."

Windflower took the corporal's hand and slapped his back. "Thank you, Harry. I really appreciate it. You're a good Mountie and a loyal friend."

Inspector Quigley went to the detachment to close it up for the night. He would meet up with Sheila and Windflower later and spend the night.

The last few people were leaving for the evening, giving Herb and Moira Stoodley and Sheila and Windflower a couple of quiet moments together to say goodnight. Then, arm in arm, Windflower and Sheila walked back home. The night was still clear and crisp, and the moon and stars shone over Grand Bank as brightly as ever before.

"Thank you, Sergeant," said Sheila. "I think you just saved Christmas."

"You are welcome, Madam Mayor. But I think I had a lot of help from my friends and the people here in Grand Bank. I'm glad that I was able to do something for a place that's brought me so much joy. I have the best gift of all. You. Merry Christmas, my love.

"Merry Christmas, Sergeant Windflower."

Melissa Nguyen

Esther Wan

A Brother for Christmas

$\mathcal{I}$ had not always welcomed the entry of my younger brother, Sean, to our family. Up until that point I was the baby, the focus of all attention, the only boy, the chosen one. Now it appeared that I would have to share centre stage. Even on the occasion of his birth, he began to interfere with my life.

He was born just before my First Holy Communion, a seminal event in the life of a Catholic boy in St. John's, a day of great reverence and celebration. Well, that's what the priest and the teachers said. I only knew that on that special day you got dressed up and wore a white ribbon to signify the event and that people gave you money you could spend on anything you wanted. Your mother's job was to bring you around to all her friends and neighbours. Your job was to act shy and take the money.

Unfortunately for me, my mother was just home from the hospital with my brother and couldn't accompany me on my rounds. I did go on my own to a few of our close neighbours on my street, but I knew it wasn't the same without the introduction from my mother. I came home depressed. I figured my brother cost me at least five dollars that day alone. That was a lot of chips and candy.

As he grew from the baby stage to toddler, my resentment grew as well. He proceeded to grow this luxurious mop of curly blond hair that all the other mothers swooned over. He even got sick, which was the final straw for me. I think he had some irregular kind of brain wave that had to be corrected, but I was sure he was just looking for attention. Once he became mobile, he also became my competitor.

He would try to mimic what I did, which wasn't always the smartest thing for him to do, as we found out with the Shirriff jelly fiasco. Years ago, the old Shirriff company had a promotion on NHL hockey coins. Every jelly package came with an NHL coin featuring a hockey player's picture and team logo. The coins quickly became sought-after possessions for all the boys in my neighbourhood. Luckily for me, Shirriff was one of the product lines that my dad's company carried, and whenever there was a broken box, he or one of the other workers got to take it home.

This meant that we had a continuous supply of jelly and always had unopened packages lying around. We only had jelly maybe twice a week, and I was much too impatient to wait around to get my hockey coins doled out in such a piecemeal fashion. So I would sneak into the cupboard, open the packages and take out the coins. Of course I got caught, but by that time, I already had the stash.

I never really noticed it, but my kid brother, who was about three at the time, had been watching my stealth adventure, and one morning he tried to beat me to the punch. He got up earlier than anybody else and snuck into the kitchen. He had to climb on a chair and then the counter to reach the top shelf where Mom had stashed all the new jelly packages. He stretched and stretched, up on his tippytoes . . . . All I heard was the howl and my mother's feet scrambling to the kitchen. He had fallen off the counter, and later we learned that he had broken his arm. I felt badly for him, until Mom started to berate me for showing my younger brother a bad example. I could swear that I saw him give a brief smile from beneath his tears.

So I guess it's fair to say that my relationship with my baby brother didn't start out well. But there were some good points to having him around. First of all, instead of me getting hauled around everywhere by my sisters, he inherited that job. Secondly, when it came time for the big Christmas trip downtown, he was selected as my mother's companion. Though this was a reminder of my subservient role as an older brother, I realized I preferred to go downtown with my buddies rather than Mom and spend time with them at the library after school.

Besides, Christmas was coming and all the world was white and wonderful. I remember becoming more and more interested in what Mom brought home from her Christmas expeditions but was just as quickly shooed away and told to mind my own business.

The Christmas after he broke his arm, I tried to pump Sean for information when he returned from the annual shopping adventure, but he was only interested in telling me about his French fries and the turkeys in the window on Water Street. Obviously a little more detailed espionage would have to be undertaken if I was to find out what Santa had in store for me.

I waited for the right opportunity to arise, and it came more quickly than I had anticipated. The following night both my parents were going to the Christmas concert at my sisters' school. One of my sisters, Brenda I think, was singing in a group of nine girls–they were known as the Triple Trios. It was a school night, and my oldest sister, Marg, stayed home to keep an eye on me and my little brother and to make sure I did my homework.

But I wasn't the only one scheming. My middle sister, Moreen, had made plans to meet up with her boyfriend, Sam, a goalie on one of the high school hockey teams, after my parents were gone. I was sworn to secrecy about her rendezvous, but I didn't care since I had a plan of my own.

Once Moreen had left and Sean was put to bed, I saw my chance. Marg, ever the studious one, was busy working in the kitchen, and I snuck into my parents' bedroom where I was sure the Christmas loot was stored. I looked under the beds and behind the dressers, but there was nothing. That left only the big brown armoire with the glass mirror on the front. I opened the doors carefully and hoped that Marg wouldn't hear the squeaking.

I dug underneath the coats and clothes and found the buried treasure: a bright red fire truck with a flashing light, siren and a hose that really sprayed water, and what looked like to me to be a real fireman's hat. I couldn't believe it.

I had always wanted a fireman's set, and now I was going to get it for Christmas. But was I? Suddenly the fears and doubts crept in. Maybe it wasn't for me. I dug a little deeper into the Christmas pile, and there were my usual Christmas presents: a brand new hockey stick and puck. The fireman's stuff was for Sean, not me. I was devastated and even went to bed before my bedtime. Marg checked my forehead to see if I was sick since I'd never been known to go to bed without being told to before. I tossed and turned but finally drifted off to sleep.

The best part about being a kid is that every day is a new adventure, and no matter what happened yesterday, all is forgotten or forgiven when you wake up in the morning. It was two days before Christmas and the last day at school before our Christmas break. There was snow on the ground and street hockey on the agenda. The next two days were a bit of a happy blur, which is usually the case during my favourite time of the year.

Finally, it was Christmas morning, and Sean was poking me in the ribs and almost screaming that Santa had come. It must have been 5 a.m. There wasn't a sound other than pleasant snores coming from the other inhabitants of the house. I shushed Sean, and together we crept out to the living room to see what Santa had brought.

"I got a fireman's set," he shouted and put on his red hat and started wheeling his fire engine around. He was about to show me the siren when I grabbed his hand and shushed him once again. Then he did a remarkable thing. He looked at me, smiled and said, "Would you like to play fireman with me?"

I could have cried and died on the spot. "Yes, yes," I said. Soon we were chasing each other around the living room, and then with him on my back, we took turns aiming the firehose and pretending we were really fighting a blazing inferno. I don't think I had ever had more fun in my life. When my parents finally got up an hour later, Sean and I were sitting at the kitchen table. I had gotten both us a bowl of cereal, and we were laughing and talking to each other. I am sure Mom and Dad were surprised by our sudden friendship. I know I was.

Now that our parents were up, there was no need to pretend to be quiet anymore, and we certainly didn't. The sound of the blaring siren and the flashing red light got my sisters out of bed in a hurry, and soon everyone was stuffing themselves on candy and Cracker Jack treats and enjoying the bounty of another Christmas together.

There would be many more times for Sean and I to play and laugh (and fight) together in the years to come, but as I looked at him that Christmas morning, I realized, maybe for the first time, that I had a brother. I had someone who I could just enjoy and love, not only at Christmas but for the rest of my life. I had received the best gift of all, a brother, for Christmas.

Ardin Edwards

First Christmas
on Calver Avenue

They had found each other by chance and circumstance. She had escaped the grinding poverty of a small fishing community by fleeing to St. John's for a position as a housekeeper. He had left a slightly larger fishing village, Trepassey, to try to become a priest.

Sadie found herself a virtual prisoner in the mansion where she cleaned and cooked. Mike's money to pay for his tuition and college fees had long run out, and he was forced to leave the seminary. He managed to find work in the warehouse of one of the great merchant companies of St. John's, Gerald S. Doyle.

They worked long, hard hours at their jobs with only Saturday afternoon and Sunday to look after their personal and religious needs. Mike had a room and board with his cousin Bride on Patrick Street. Bride Martin's was the drop-in centre for all the refugees from St. Mary's Bay, and most of them stopped in regularly for a cup of tea and news from home, which came via the taxi drivers who ferried people back and forth.

Romance was hardly the first thing that either Mike or Sadie thought of. He was a painfully shy, thirty-something bachelor, and she had long since given up on the idea of getting married. But Bride Martin saw the loneliness of the two of them and nudged one and poked the other until Mike finally got up the courage to ask Sadie out on a date. She agreed, and they went to the movies at the Nickel Theatre in the Benevolent Irish Society building on Queen's Road.

After the movies he took her to the Fountain Spray store on Military Road across from Government House where they ate custard cones and waited until the lights came on in the fountain before he walked her back home. Soon they were a regular couple and had weekly dates that sometimes included a dance at the American air force base in Fort Pepperrell or at the Knights of Columbus. With Bride's encouragement Mike proposed and Sadie accepted. After a four-week period in which their intentions to marry were announced at Mass every Sunday, they were married in the small chapel at the back of St. Patrick's church.

It was a small wedding and an even smaller reception back at Bride Martin's. Eight other couples and a handful of relatives, including Sadie's father and brother Pat and Mike's brother Leo, enjoyed cold turkey, ham, salads and homemade rolls. There were two bottles of whisky purchased for the big event, carefully rationed and out of sight until Bride determined it was time for another round.

For entertainment someone brought out an accordion, and with little encouragement, all the couples were soon dancing and singing so loud that Bride had to shush them for fear of offending the neighbours. The only real incident occurred when Pat, Sadie's brother who had ignored Bride's mini-temperance rules by procuring his own bottle of rum, crashed into the kitchen table while performing his own rather indelicate tap dance routine. But nothing could really spoil the day for the newly married couple, and later in life Sadie would tell people that this had been the happiest day of her life.

The newlyweds bid goodbye to their friends and family just after ten o'clock to go to their new apartment and begin their married life together. They got a ride from Sadie's cousin, one of the St. Mary's Bay taxi drivers, to Suvla Street near Empire Avenue. Their basement apartment was small, cramped and dingy, but for them it was a little bit of paradise.

The soft summer days passed too quickly as the damp foggy days of autumn turned into the cold slog of winter. Mike rose early in the morning to walk the two miles to work in the warehouse at Doyle's on Blackmarsh Road. Sadie would follow soon after on her way to her job as a domestic helper. Stirring in Sadie's head was the idea that somehow, some way, they would one day be able to have a real house of their own.

Also stirring inside of Sadie was Margaret, their first born, and by spring it was no secret to anyone. In May she was finally born to the great relief and celebration of her parents. Sadie stayed home with Margaret for the rest of the year, but now more than ever, she was determined to find a place for her small family. Days and weeks and months passed quickly as Sadie and Mike watched and enjoyed their new blessing grow.

The Martins's apartment on Suvla Street became another gathering place for the wayward from St. Mary's Bay, lost in the hustle and bustle of big St. John's and longing for a connection to home. Games of cards on a Saturday evening, ham sandwiches on Sunday night, and a single bottle of rye whisky, doled out on a drink-by-drink basis, made up their entertainment. Two and half years later, their second daughter, Moreen, was born just before Christmas. By now Sadie was fixated on getting out of their basement apartment to have a real home built.

Mike and Sadie had no money for a down payment, and with Mike's meagre salary from Doyle's, they had little standing with the bank to get a mortgage. The only way that families like them could get assistance from the banks was through the intervention of their employer. For months now Sadie had been badgering Mike to talk to Mr. Doyle to get his blessing, and for the same months Mike had been dodging the issue. Finally, much to Mike's dismay and embarrassment, Sadie called the office and arranged an appointment with the boss.

When Mike found out, his usual cool demeanour vanished, and he was furious with his wife. He didn't strike out in anger; that wasn't his style. He was more of the brooding, simmering kind. Eventually, though, he came around to the idea, which was a good thing since their meeting with old Mr. Doyle was scheduled for after work that Saturday morning. On Saturday Mike was called to the office to see his wife standing there in her Sunday best, clutching her handbag in nervous anticipation.

But by the time they got to the boss's office, Sadie's determination showed through, and she thoroughly charmed the old man into not only calling the bank on their behalf but to lend them the down payment that Mike would repay through deductions from his weekly paycheque. It was not unusual for benevolent employers to assist their workers in this way, at a fairly high rate of interest of course, and Sadie and Mike left the office with their dreams alive and their hopes high.

Almost immediately Sadie started scouring the area where they lived for their new home and before long had her heart set on a small yellow bungalow on nearby Calver Avenue. There was a short brown fence in front and a large backyard out back, and she couldn't wait to tell Mike about it when he came home from work. After supper all four of the Martin family headed up the road to take a closer look. Mike was as smitten as Sadie, and it took a bit of scheming to figure out how they could afford the payments.

The only choice they had was to rent out part of the house, and since it had no basement, they would have to split the house into two sections. That was fairly easy since there was a natural split between the front and back of the house, and all rooms had doors, affording privacy. They would have to share the bathroom with another family, but that seemed like a small price to pay to stop paying rent and start building up an ownership stake for themselves.

Sadie did all the legwork in dealing with Doyle's and the bank, and she even found another young couple, John and Violet Bulger, who were from Mike's hometown of Trepassey, to take the front half of the house and thereby split the expenses.

By June the Martins were lugging their few possessions up the hill to 41 Calver Avenue, and by July they were enjoying sitting under the shady trees in their very own backyard.

With two small children Sadie was now at home full-time while Mike trudged off to Blackmarsh Road every morning. She spent her time and energy turning the little house into their home. Soon winter came and so did the Christmas season. They didn't have much to give each other or their children that Christmas, but they had a lot to be grateful for. Early on Christmas Eve Sadie sent Mike off to Churchill Square to get their very first Christmas tree while she thawed their small turkey in a bowl under the kitchen table. When he got home, she took out her few boxes of Christmas ornaments, one string of lights and a single box of tinsel that she had picked up for half price at the Arcade the year before, and with much joy on the faces of their two little daughters, they happily decorated the tree. When Mike plugged in the lights, the girls laughed and squealed and shrieked at this miracle. To them and to Mike and Sadie, too, it seemed like the Eiffel Tower in Paris. And it was.

Later that evening Mike went off to midnight Mass at the Basilica while Sadie watched the girls sleep. She thought about how far they had come to get here and how fortunate they were. When Mike came home, cold but happy, with a dusting of snow on his Sunday fedora, they had a late snack and headed off to bed to wait for the arrival of their first Christmas morning on Calver Avenue.

Three more children would come in the years ahead, and before too long the Bulgers would move out of the house to begin their own journey. Mike and Sadie would live in this little house on Calver Avenue for nearly sixty more years, and for all the joys that would come, nothing would ever top that very first Christmas on Calver Avenue.

Alysa Wong

Jennifer Fancy

Christmas Lights

Christmas as a child growing up in St. John's in the fifties and sixties was always a wonderful, magical time of the year. We didn't have much, but it seemed like no one did, so we didn't worry about it. We weren't expecting much for Christmas, but that didn't lessen our anticipation or enthusiasm for the event. There were few television commercials to tempt us and even fewer stores to press our noses up against. That didn't slow us down though. There was just something about Christmas that made everything special.

Sometimes I wonder if Christmas was enjoyed more back then because life, and therefore Christmas, was much slower and simpler. But when I see the absolute joy in children's eyes today at Christmastime, I realize that that's not it. They enjoy their Christmas every bit as much as we did "back in the day." And just like us, if you took away all of the trappings and just gave a little bit of snow and a few twinkling lights, they'd still love Christmas all the same.

Ah, the twinkling lights. That is one of my dearest memories from Christmases past, and something I look forward to even today, although I have to admit that starting in early November and electrifying the neighbourhood à la Griswold is a bit much, even for me. And what is it with these white lights? People, Christmas is about colour, red and green preferably, but I acknowledge yellow and blue as acceptable. I can even stretch to not disdain the mauves and oranges and those beyond the normal spectrum. But white is not a colour, and colour is an essential element of my Christmas.

That love of Christmas colour started early in life, as far back as my earliest memories. As soon as I was big enough, in the determination of my parents, I was allowed to go on the annual tour of Christmas lights. This was a big event whereby my siblings – three older sisters – and I, accompanied by our father, would take a bus ride all over St. John's to bear witness to people's love affair with Christmas lights.

We took the bus because we didn't have a car, or a lot of money. My father didn't make much working for Gerald S. Doyle, one of the city's wealthiest merchant families. Doyle had made his money first supplying fishermen and then catering to the growing Newfoundland population by selling them back their own product in the form of cod liver oil pills. Dad worked in the warehouse on Blackmarsh Road, just up from the Purity factory, and he didn't seem to mind walking back and forth to work from our little house on Calver Avenue.

Other than an occasional bus ride back up from shopping downtown on Water Street, this was the bus ride of the year. It would probably be a few days before Christmas when my father would make the announcement that the following night we would be going to see "The Lights." I still remember my first year. I was six and in grade two, and I was overjoyed when it became clear that I would be joining the entourage. My two oldest sisters had begged off, but my youngest sister, Brenda, and I were happy to be going along.

After school I rushed home and waited in the window for Dad to appear. He arrived just after 5:30, a light snow dusting his long overcoat and black fedora. Supper was very quickly put on the table and gone within minutes. After supper he sat in his chair and read the paper for a few minutes while I kept watch on him and the time. Around half past six Dad rose and announced that it was time. I was ready to go with my boots on in a flash.

The three of us headed out the door. My mother for some reason begged off and did not accompany us, but both Brenda and I were oblivious to the fact that there were other adults in the world besides Dad. We walked out, bundled up in mitts, scarves and hats, and walked the short distance from our house up to Merrymeeting Road where we waited for the bus. Before long the blue bus pulled up to our stop and Dad paid our fare. I think it was twenty-five cents for adults and ten for kids, and he got me on for nothing because I was so little. Brenda and I ran to the back of the bus and got the very back bench seat, the one with windows all around.

The first and last thing I remember about the bus in St. John's was that it was hot, like four hundred degrees hot. After coming in wrapped like a mummy in layers and sitting in sauna-like conditions for two minutes, Brenda and I were both soaked. So, very quickly, we peeled off our outer layers until finally we sat, wide-eyed but comfortable, in our tee shirts staring out the windows at the blinking and shimmering outside.

As we rode around, almost every house had some form of light acknowledging the season, and this appeared to be the case regardless of the neighbourhood, poor or rich. Even the curmudgeons had some lights, usually those red-candle-in-a-wreath lights that made it look like they were having a funeral rather than a celebration. The real difference in the quality and quantity of Christmas colour really seemed to depend on enthusiasm rather than income, although the very rich had an opulence of Christmas lights that was designed to impress, and it certainly did that for two little kids like my sister and me.

The bus took us on a route through the centre of town, across Lemarchant Road, which only in St. John's could turn into a whole bunch of others streets: Cornwall Avenue, Hamilton Avenue and then Topsail Road. This area was not particularly well-to-do, but its residents were comfortable, and maybe because they were on such a busy roadway, they made a special effort to show off. We saw Santa and his reindeer in various modes of transit and motion, and several nativity scenes from elaborate to obviously homemade. We enjoyed them all equally well.

Most people modestly had two or three strings of lights, those big, fat outdoor lights that were so popular in the days before we realized they were energy suckers. They would string the lights along their eaves and maybe around the front windows as well. Many kept their lights high from the ground so the neighbourhood vandals wouldn't steal them, something I never attempted of course. Sometimes, when you went out in the morning, you'd see that all the lights in a string near the ground were missing. You'd find fragments of them smashed in the snowy streets nearby. That's all I know about it, honest.

The highlight of the trip was when the bus swung down from Topsail Road to Waterford Bridge Road via a great little road called Road De Luxe. This abutted the archbishop's residence and its massive grounds showing how highly the Roman Catholic Church thought of itself. We swung along the road toward Bowering Park and up toward what we insensitively called "The Mental." The unfortunate reference was to a hospital, and while we were certainly afraid to venture an inch up the driveway, there was always a beautiful crèche scene at the front of the building.

Having reached the halfway point of our journey, we then travelled up Cowan Avenue, which was the de facto city limits for St. John's. Somewhere beyond was Mount Pearl, a much smaller community back then than it is today, and not much else. Cowan Avenue brought another string of big homes and flashy light displays that made heading in the direction of home at least bearable. We then went down Topsail Road and past "The San," the local sanatorium where people with TB were basically locked up until they weren't contagious anymore. Tuberculosis was still a big health threat back then, and the authorities and all the rest of us took it pretty seriously.

We retraced our steps over the winding roads that led us back to the area known as the Higher Levels. We were just a few streets from home, but first there was a treasured stop before the end of our magical evening. We got off at a small takeout that served delicious soft-serve ice cream we called custard cones. It was a fitting treat to cap a night of light and wonder. We trundled back the last few minutes with smiles on our faces and pure joy in our hearts. That night my sleep was filled with Christmas, more Christmas, and even more Christmas.

Christmas Eve and Christmas Day were still to come, and they were eagerly anticipated. But somehow after we had finished our trip to see the lights, I felt that I had received the best gift of all. The lights would flicker and glow for the whole twelve days of Christmas, and then they would linger in my heart until the season rolled around again.

In later years when we had a car, the bus adventure disappeared, but we still did a tour of the lights in Dad's new Rambler. This wasn't nearly the same, but having a car allowed us to travel a little farther, including out on Empire Avenue West. That's where one special man had created his own personal version of an electric Christmas, complete with Santa, all the reindeer and a full cast of Disney holiday characters. But somehow it wasn't the same or as much fun as that hot, stuffy and very happy bus ride.

I still love the Christmas lights today and not just for the memories. I like the fact that in the depths of darkness we can string a few bulbs together and create a magical feeling where, at least for a few days, we are grateful for what we have and want to share it with others. Isn't that the real spirit of Christmas?

Gotta go now. It's time to put the lights up. Merry Christmas.

Jamie Pomeroy

Tizzard's Christmas Dream

Eddie Tizzard tried to wake up, but it was like he was tied down. Must be the medication, he thought. He hated the sensation; he could hardly feel himself and he couldn't move. Then he realized he was dreaming. He'd had lots of strange dreams lately – the medication, again.

In this dream he was a little kid in Ramea, maybe five years old. His mom was in the kitchen, and he was playing underneath the kitchen table. His older brother Sean was having a discussion with his mother. Well, it was more like an argument. Sean wanted to sign up for the military, and his mother was having none of it.

"Wait 'til your da' gets home," she said. "He'll put you straight."

His brother walked away in a huff, and he could hear his mother mutter as she pounded whatever was in her mixing bowl.

"Well, that fixes that," little Eddie said to himself.

But it didn't fix anything, because later, after Eddie had gone to bed, he could hear more loud voices and yelling, most of it from Sean and his mother. His dad was, as usual, trying to keep the peace. At the end of the yelling, he heard a door bang and hushed whispers in the kitchen. He drifted off to sleep and found out in the morning that his brother was in fact heading off to the army. Within weeks he would be gone.

The Tizzards would see Sean one more time. After basic training in Gagetown, he managed to get a week's leave to spend Christmas at home with his family. Eddie remembered it as one of his best Christmases ever. But he also felt the sadness that was underneath it, knowing that his older brother would be going away to a place called Afghanistan soon after.

Everything after that was a blur in young Eddie's memory. After they all went to the wharf and waved goodbye to Sean with his boots all shiny and his knapsack over his shoulder, things became very quiet in the Tizzard house. His mother hardly spoke at all. She kissed him goodnight with a "God bless ya" as usual, but she said almost nothing else to him, his two sisters and especially to his father, who he heard say under his breath one time something about "cold shoulder again for lunch."

That spring his parents were called to go into St.

John's to meet with the army officers at the base. The first word to trickle back to Ramea from St. John's was that Sean had been wounded in action in Afghanistan and that it sounded serious. Then a few days later, his parents came back to Ramea and sat everyone down around the kitchen table. His father spoke. His mother just quietly cried into her handkerchief. She never looked up once as Eddie's father explained how Sean had been hurt, how his Jeep had been blown up by a bomb at the side of the road, how he had died from his injuries.

"He died a hero for his country," said Eddie's father, looking right at him. "We can never forget that, or him."

After those words were spoken, his mother got up from the table and went into her bedroom. When she came out, she was dressed in black from head to toe. Eddie never saw her again in any other colour.

After a few blurry days of people visiting and Sean's body being returned by the same ferry that had taken him away, it was all over.

Later that year, his mom took sick, and on Christmas Eve, she died. People whispered that she died of a broken heart and wanted to be with her son in heaven. Some days Eddie wished that for himself, too. But that didn't happen, and Eddie Tizzard's life was changed forever.

His father was attentive and caring, and his sisters

were kind and comforting, but he could never find a place of peace inside his little soul. It felt too empty, and he felt too alone. He was still feeling that way in his dream when he felt a stirring and heard a familiar voice.

"Good morning, and Merry Christmas, Eddie. Breakfast time. You don't want to miss a meal now, do ya?"

Eddie pushed his way up from the bottom of his sleep world and blinked his eyes to see if they still worked. Eddie reached over to grab his father's hand. "Good morning, Dad."

His father smiled at his son's voice. It wasn't too long ago that Eddie could not speak and could hardly move. He had nearly lost his life after being shot near Stephenville.

"Scrambled eggs and toast with a nice piece of honeydew melon. Doesn't get any better than that around here b'y."

"I'd love a big thick piece of fried bologna," said Eddie. "That would be some good b'y."

This was the way that the father and son often started their day, talking about the foods they loved as they ate together. "Yes b'y, that would be great," said the older man. "Maybe we should have fried bologna instead of turkey for Christmas dinner tonight."

Richard Tizzard had become accustomed to getting his son's breakfast tray from the kitchen in the clinic and bringing it over to Eddie personally. The cook often gave him a second tray for himself. He wasn't a patient, but lately he was as much a regular as any of the staff.

Eddie laughed at the thought of bologna for Christmas dinner, even though it still really hurt when he laughed. Then he turned serious. "I had a dream. Mom was in it and so was Sean. Dad, why did you let him go away?"

Richard Tizzard's sparkling eyes grew dull and his face tightened. He paused and thought for a moment.

"Son, I had no more chance of stopping Sean than I could stop the wind from coming across the harbour in Ramea. He was as headstrong a young man as I have ever seen. He wanted to see the world, not read about it or have someone else tell him about it. I tried to get him to slow down, maybe go to university first. But he was impatient. Reminds me of someone else I know."

"It killed Mom," said Eddie.

"It almost killed me, too. There's not a day goes by that I don't think about both of them. But I knew that someone had to look after you and your sisters. That was my job."

He paused again and took out his handkerchief to blow his nose.

"Sometimes late at night when everybody is gone to sleep and the whole world is quiet, I talk to them," he said quietly, almost in a whisper.

"Do they ever talk back?"

"Not yet," his dad smiled, "but I do believe that they hear me. I just don't think it's possible that all there is in this world is what we can see or hear. The ocean tells me that. We can explore it all we want, but we'll never understand everything about it. It's too deep a mystery."

Richard Tizzard wanted to speak about happier times, especially happier times yet to come.

"Enough of that," he announced. "We have to get you well enough so that you can go dancing with that girl of yours on New Year's."

"I don't think that's likely, Dad. I can barely raise my arms, let alone my feet. But it will be good to see Carrie again."

"She's a great girl. If your mother were alive, she'd be marryin' you off by now. It is time, you know."

"Let's get through breakfast before we start the wedding music."

Both men laughed and dug into their eggs.

An hour later Sgt. Winston Windflower popped his head into the room at the Grand Bank Clinic. Their trays were empty, but both men were still laughing.

"What's so funny?" asked Windflower.

"Merry Christmas, Sarge. We're just happy to be alive," said Eddie. "Didn't expect to see you here. I'm honoured to have such a lovely visitor Christmas morn."

"I'll leave you two," said his father. "I got to see a man about a wild bologna."

Both Tizzards laughed again as the elder took his leave. Windflower smiled, but he had to admit he'd absolutely no clue what they were talking about. He thought about asking about the wild bologna but wisely left that alone.

"Jones has gone to St. John's to pick Carrie up," said Windflower. "I think she managed to get on the only flight landing in the province. The road into town is gone, so she, Frost and Carrie will be making part of the journey by snowmobile."

"Wow, it's really bad out there by the sounds of it, Sarge. I'd give anything to take on a few shifts to help out."

"Your job is to rest, Eddie. They should be here by lunchtime as long as the snow holds off."

"I heard we're getting a dump. My mother always said that it was God's gift to us to have snow at Christmastime."

"Well, she's getting her wish this year. Lots of snow out there. It might mean working a few extra shifts for me, but up until a week ago, we'd had an easy year. And with Sheila pregnant, we're not partying as much anyway."

"I just feel so useless lying around here, Sarge."

"There'll be lots of time for work, Eddie. You need to get better, first. Do you understand?"

"Yes, Sir."

"Do you need anything?"

"Nah, I'm good. I'm just impatient."

"Well, we finally got you to slow down," said Windflower, laughing as he left his young friend.

"Very funny," said Eddie, mostly to himself.

The psychologist who had come to see him earlier had told him that one of the hardest parts about a long recovery was staying positive and patient. Staying positive was easy. When he got down, he just kept in mind that he didn't have long to wait before his dad or Windflower would pop by to cheer him up again. The patient thing, though, was another matter. But maybe that's why they call me a patient, he thought. I have to take my time.

He was still pondering that idea when the nurse came in to help him with his physio for the day. That took his mind off everything. It was hard work keeping his legs from completely degenerating while strengthening his upper body. He was exhausted afterwards and drifted back off into a sound sleep until he heard a familiar voice.

"Eddie, how are you?"

Carrie Evanchuk was sitting on the chair next to his bed when he opened his eyes. Her wide smile lit up the room, and Eddie smiled, too, despite his discomfort.

"Fine, fine," said Eddie. "Just a little beat-up from the physio that's supposed to help me get back on my feet. How long have you been here?"

"Yvette dropped me off a few minutes ago. I saw you stir and moan. I wanted to make sure you were okay."

"Yeah, yeah, I'm good," said Eddie, pulling himself into a sitting position.

"Really? You look stressed out of your brain. You must be going crazy being laid up like this."

Eddie shrugged. "I think I'm going to take up meditation," he deadpanned.

Evanchuk started to react and then saw the smile start to grow across his face. They both laughed out loud at the same time.

"What's so funny?" asked Eddie's dad as he walked into the room with his son's lunch tray.

"Hi Carrie, nice to see you," Richard Tizzard said. "You won't be laughing when you see the pitifully small lunch they gave you," he said to his son.

He held up a small bowl of greenish soup, two crackers, a half ham sandwich and a tiny cup of jello. "A man could starve on that. Luckily, I stopped by the Mug-Up and Moira was there and opened up for me, bless her. She got us a couple of turkey sandwiches."

Then, turning to Carrie, he asked, "Have you eaten? I can go back and get you something too, if you'd like."

"No thanks, Sir," said Evanchuk. "Yvette Jones met me at the airport and had a care package all ready for me. I love to watch other people eat, though. It reminds me of being home with my brothers."

"In that case, we're happy to oblige," said the older Tizzard, and he passed a sandwich over to Eddie and sat in the other chair to eat his own.

The trio spent a happy hour together while the two men ate their lunch and Evanchuk told them of her adventures on the RCMP security detail in Ottawa. She would be staying with Constable Jones until New Year's. The nurse came in to clear the tray and give Eddie his medications. He took them and started to drowse.

"I'm glad you were able to come," said Richard Tizzard to Evanchuk as they left Eddie's room so he could nap. "He's been a bit down. He could use the company of a woman, instead of his old man."

"I'm sure he loves having you around," said Evanchuk. "He is always talking about how nice you are. He really loves you."

"I think he's pretty fond of you, too. He was counting down the days 'til you got here."

The pair hugged before going their separate ways.

Eddie Tizzard truly was happy to see Carrie again and relieved. Once he had regained consciousness in the Stephenville hospital, he had doubted himself and his ability to recover. Not only that, he had wondered if Carrie would want to stick around and continue to be part of his life. But, here he was now, finishing his convalescence in Grand Bank, and Carrie Evanchuk was here, too, to share Christmas with him. He was a lucky man.

With that thought, he let himself drift into a deep sleep and began another dream.

Again, it was Christmas all those years ago, and he was standing outside his old house in Ramea. His mother was standing at the kitchen table. It was like old times, but something was different. His mother was dressed all in black, except for a single white ribbon on her breast.

"Hello, my son," she said.

"Mom," said Eddie. "What's going on?"

"Didn't you call me?"

"You can hear me?"

"Only when you really need me. I was with you in Stephenville. But you were pretty out of it."

"Yeah, I guess so. I thought I was dreaming when you came."

"You were," said his mother.

"I guess I'm a little down right now. I try to keep my spirits up for Dad."

"He's doing the same for you."

"I guess I'm not sure about the future. What will happen to me? Will I be okay? What should I do? Maybe I'm just confused."

"Maybe. All I really know is what we have is today, this moment. The past is what we believe it to be. The future is what we hope it will become. What we do today influences both."

"Now you're talking like Dad."

"He's not the only smart one in the family." She paused, her voice becoming quieter. "I have some regrets," she said, "things I wished I had said and done. I got so busy dealing with a future that could never come and a past that I wanted to change that I forgot about today."

"Mom, it was hard losing Sean."

"It was. But I also lost Richard and you, Margaret and Brenda. In the end I even lost myself. But I'm at peace with that now. I see Sean sometimes."

"What does he say?" asked Eddie.

"He keeps wondering why you're not marrying that nice girl who's head over heels in love with you."

"She is?"

"Everybody in the world can see it but you."

"But I'm lying here in bed, not knowing if I can ever get out. Who would want to be with someone like that?"

"That's not up to you, Eddie. We all have our own paths to follow. That might be hers. At least she is prepared to choose it because she thinks it might be right for her. And for you, too."

"How do you know if it's right or not?"

"You don't. But the good thing about it is that you get to choose. If you don't go through that door, another one will open. But the first door may never be there again. You just don't know."

Then Eddie felt himself being drawn back toward the light. He had many more questions to ask his mother, but she faded as the light appeared, and he woke up. He found himself staring out the window, watching the first of very fat flakes fall to the ground. Beautiful, he thought.

"Christmas snow," said his dad who had quietly entered his room. He had two cups of tea on a tray with two plates of turkey, dressing, mashed potatoes, vegetables, cranberries and lots of gravy. It was a quiet Christmas meal but shared with love between a father and son. After dinner, they spent an hour playing cribbage. With the daylight gone, the Christmas lights all over Grand Bank sparkled and twinkled in the falling snow.

That evening was a quiet one with visits by Sheila and Windflower, and Evanchuk and Jones who stayed until Eddie Tizzard's next round of medications. Once Eddie started to look sleepy, they said goodnight. Jones left first, and Evanchuk hung around to hold his hand as he drifted off. She kissed him goodnight and turned out the lights.

That night Eddie had lots of dreams, but no

special visitors, and he woke up feeling alive and very refreshed in the morning. He was surprised when his dad didn't show up for breakfast. The morning nurse was very pleasant when she brought him in his tray, a tray with a particularly small breakfast, but no, she hadn't seen Richard Tizzard that morning.

It was still snowing, maybe even heavier this morning, and many people had left their Christmas lights on. Eddie could see some of them from his window. He could also see that something was happening in the clinic parking lot. In fact, there was a lot happening in the clinic parking lot. The first thing to grab his attention wasn't what he saw, but what he heard. It was a band playing Christmas music, not just any band but the Grand Bank Salvation Army Marching Band, their red uniforms getting spattered with a few fat flakes, their silver instruments glinting in the morning light.

To Eddie's great surprise, they marched right by, the band major saluting in the direction of Eddie's window. Then came a flatbed truck with a choir of children from the nearby school who stopped right in front and sang O Holy Night, Eddie's favourite Christmas song. How did they know that, he thought? Then, he saw his father in the back of a rented convertible, and he knew that this was no coincidence.

Soon afterwards came all the RCMP vehicles with his old buddies, and even his boss, Inspector Ron

Quigley from Marystown. They all had their lights flashing, and in the final vehicle, the vintage fire truck from the Grand Bank Volunteer Fire Department, was the Mayor of Grand Bank, Sheila Hillier, and the true guest of honour, Santa Claus. All the participants in this impromptu parade waved to Eddie as he watched in stunned disbelief.

Windflower came into his room with the nurse. "You missed the parade last week," he said, "so we wanted to give you a little taste. Speaking of taste, we have something else."

The nurse checked the side rails on Eddie's bed, making sure they were secure, and then she and Windflower rolled him out of the room and down the corridor toward another set of surprises. Eddie saw Carrie first. Then he noticed all of his RCMP friends and dozens of other local townspeople. They had come to wish Eddie a Merry Christmas.

"We know you can't get out, but we all want you and your dad to have a special Christmas," said Sheila, who was one of the first to greet him.

Eddie was half sitting up in totally stunned silence when he saw Herb and Moira Stoodley wheel in a table full of food. There was a turkey, a ham, potatoes and gravy and dressing, and on the end with a red ribbon tied around it was a full plate of fried bologna with his name written on it. There was also a full tray of cookies and tarts and what looked like a coconut cream cheesecake, Eddie's favourite. He started to smile – and to eat. Boy, did he eat. He had a little of everything and a big piece of fried bologna.

He only stopped eating when the crowd of people parted to let a ragged-looking group of people into the lobby. It was mummers who had decided to start their Boxing Day excursions here at the Grand Bank Clinic. "Dis a special hoccassion," the chief mummer – or maybe just the loudest – shouted, "on da safe return of da prodigal son of Grand Bank, Eddie Tizzard."

He also announced that they would even perform without getting their usual free drink of rum. That prompted the other mummers to push him aside and start singing and dancing all around. They soon had everyone clapping and singing along with them, and even the clinic staff who'd come to watch were soon part of the action. After a few tunes on a fiddle that one of them had brought along, accompanied by a combination of ugly sticks, cow bells, combs and what looked like part of an old washing machine, they made their way out into the parking lot and were gone.

The last part of the agenda for the morning was a visit from Santa. The fat, jolly man, who Eddie suspected was Evan Shortall, the plow operator, would soon have to get back to work. He gave Eddie a sackful of gifts and chocolates and told him that even though he'd been pretty naughty, Santa would give him a break this year. But next year he'd have to do better, much better.

The crowd thinned after Santa left, and the snow continued to fall outside. The RCMP crew were all getting ready for a long day and night ahead. Eddie shook as many hands as he could and was then wheeled back to his room by the nurse accompanied by Windflower, Carrie and his dad.

"Thank you all so very much," said Eddie. "I know that you all had a hand in this, and I really appreciate it. It's good to be home and with you."

Windflower smiled and shook his hand goodbye. "Sheila and I will be by later. I've got to get our storm watch organized."

"I'm gone, too," said his father. "I've got to see Brenda and Margaret and their families, but I'll be back later."

That left only Carrie and Eddie.

"You must be exhausted," she said. "I should leave, too."

"I am, but it's a pleasure. As Shakespeare once said, 'Pleasure and action make the hours seem short.' Please stay for a few minutes."

"Okay," said Carrie, sitting down in a chair opposite Eddie. "I didn't know you knew Shakespeare."

"Been practising with my dad. I'm glad we can be alone, Carrie. I need to ask you something."

"Sure, go ahead."

"Why are you here? I mean, I know you are here because we're going out together. But if I were you, I would've run away so fast . . . "

"I don't think so, Eddie. You would be right here in this chair. I know that for sure. You are the most loyal person I know. I am too, and that's part of why I'm here, but it's more than that. I thought we had something special."

"We did," said Eddie. "But that was before all this. I'm not sure when I'm getting out of here. I can't even get out of bed. I'm not sure that I have anything to offer you anymore."

"You're still you, Eddie. Don't try and push me away. We have lots of time, and I'm happy to wait as long as it takes. I love you, Eddie."

"I love you, too, Carrie. I just wanted to give you the chance to walk away, But I'm really glad you didn't. I'm going to work as hard as I can to get back to where I was and to where we were."

The two embraced as the snow outside piled up. "This is Christmastime snow," he said. "The most magical snow of the year. And I am the most blessed man in Grand Bank. Merry Christmas, my love."

"Merry Christmas, Eddie."

Anna Brimacombe-Tanner

Jessica Ellis

The Christmas Miracle

*I*t had been a long year and everybody at the Grand Bank RCMP Detachment was ready for a break. They were just finishing up their Christmas lunch, sitting around in the pleasant haze that accompanies good food and good friends.

They had eaten Sheila's seafood lasagna as well as a full turkey dinner Betsy had brought over from home and that her husband, Bob, had served up for everybody. There were salads galore and a full stack of pies and cookies that people from the neighbourhood had kept dropping off at the office all week.

"I'm stuffed," said Sergeant Winston Windflower.

"Like a turkey," replied Corporal Eddie Tizzard. Everyone groaned a little, but they still laughed at Tizzard's joke.

It was two days before Christmas and some of them would be scrambling on their way to holiday locations in the next few hours. Tizzard and his fiancée, Carrie Evanchuk, were going to Saskatchewan to meet her parents for the first time. When he was asked if he was nervous about that, Tizzard said, "Not really, except for her six big brothers."

Constable Yvette Jones was heading to Nova Scotia for her first family Christmas in years. She, too, was a little anxious, since she'd asked fellow Mountie Harry Frost to go with her. They weren't engaged, yet. But their fling while he was in Grand Bank had turned out to be much of a thing. They were still trying to figure out exactly what that was, since he was in Manitoba and she was still in Grand Bank. But it was something.

And they wanted to be together at Christmas.

Windflower and Constable Rick Smithson would be holding the fort in Grand Bank over the holidays. He would have rather had the time off to be with his wife Sheila and their new baby, Amelia Louise, but this year it was his turn to work through Christmas. He didn't mind the work, but Windflower hated missing anything with his wife and their baby.

The biggest change in their little creature was her ability to move. She could push up to a crawl, motor to where she wanted and grab what she needed. She could even stand up while holding onto the end table in the living room and inch along with one hand free to capture whatever got her attention. That wasn't always good, as Windflower discovered when she managed to get a handful of Sheila's three-layer dip before he could catch her.

"I only left her for a second," was his feeble plea for clemency from Sheila, who was not amused. "You have to be more careful," she said. "It only takes a moment for something terrible to happen. Wait 'til she gets walking."

Windflower was remorseful and tried to appear duly chastened. But he thought he could see a sneaky smile creep across Amelia Louise's face as he was getting dressed down. That girl is going to get me into trouble, he thought. But his second thought was how much he adored her. Totally worth getting in trouble for.

He loved playing with her as she focused on her blocks and patiently put them into their correct slots or holes. He just had to make sure that none of the smaller pieces ended up in her mouth. He felt like he was living on the precipice of danger and excitement all the time. He loved it. He especially loved reading her stories at bedtime and watching her as her eyes grew big at Good Night Moon, as she tried to find the hiding little mouse and as she drifted and fell so deeply to sleep that he wanted to check her breathing.

Windflower was lost in that baby heaven, probably brought about by the abundance of food and his three desserts to finish off, when he was brought back to earth by Betsy asking him a question.

"I'm sorry, Betsy, what did you say?" he asked.

"I said I was going to leave a plate of turkey in the

fridge for sandwiches, but I'm taking the rest over to the old folks' home if that's okay with you."

"Absolutely," said Windflower.

"At least the weather is good," said Tizzard as he grabbed another date square before Betsy could wrap them up.

"Should be good for going up the highway," said Windflower. "But it looks like we're going to get some snow on Christmas Eve."

"That'll be nice," said Evanchuk. "We always have snow for Christmas. In Estevan the high is around minus ten this time of year."

"Pack your long johns," said Smithson. "The wind-chill will cut you in two."

"First thing in my bag," said Tizzard. "But I don't mind the cold. My dad always says that some good comes from everything. When we had a cow back in Ramea, he would tell us that it was so cold that when he milked her, all he got was ice cream."

Everyone laughed.

"He said his dream was to have a brown cow so we could have chocolate ice cream."

This time everybody groaned.

"It will be nice to have a bit of white stuff on the ground for Christmas," said Windflower. "I just hope we only get a bit and not a big dump. That tends to drive people crazy."

"But it'll keep 'em indoors," said Smithson.

"Unless somebody decides they want to go to the hospital in the middle of the snowstorm," said Evanchuk.

"That won't happen. Will it, Boss?" asked Smithson.

"Better be prepared," said Tizzard. "Happened here a few years ago. Guy had a heart attack, or thought he was. Good luck with that."

"Luck is where opportunity meets preparation," said Windflower.

"Shakespeare?" asked Tizzard.

"Nope," said Windflower. "It's Seneca, the Roman philosopher. Good advice though."

Smithson shook his head in acknowledgement but did not appear to be reassured.

"Nothing's going to happen," said Windflower. "Nothing ever happens in Grand Bank."

Windflower groggily managed to get through the afternoon and wished his co-workers a good holiday as each of them came to say goodbye. He shook hands with all the officers and went to do the same with Betsy. But she was having none of that. She wrapped him in a big momma bear hug and kissed him on the cheek for good measure.

"You call me if you need me," said Betsy as she was leaving. "I'm just across the road b'y."

"You enjoy yourself and a Happy Christmas to you and Bob," said Windflower. "We'll be fine here."

"Okay, Sergeant, you and Sheila and that precious child have a great Christmas, too. See you in a few days," said Betsy.

Once the office had finally cleared out, Windflower had the place to himself. Smithson was out on his rounds and wouldn't likely be back for an hour or so. Windflower leaned back in his chair and decided to close his eyes just for a minute. Before he knew it, he was solidly asleep. Then he started to dream.

It was winter, so cold he shivered. The snow was swirling around him as if he were in the middle of the snowstorm's madness. He could barely see. Then faintly he could pick out an animal a little way off. He walked toward it. It was a female deer. Even though she stared at him as he got closer, she didn't appear to be afraid. As he neared, he could see her breath rise right through the blowing snow in the cold morning air.

"Look after the little ones," she whispered. She turned and ran swiftly in the snow, and a few seconds later she was gone. He didn't notice right away, but there was another figure in the shadowy morning, a much smaller one. Standing a little shakily was a fawn, not very old by the size and look of it. Windflower came closer to the baby deer, but she spooked and sprang off quickly, disappearing into the snow like her mother. He tried to follow, but it felt like he was swallowed up by the snow and lifted into the air–then dropped. He woke with a start as his office chair almost tipped over.

Wow, wonder what that means, he thought? And, he almost never dreamt in the daytime. He knew from his work with his Auntie Marie, a master dream weaver, that daytime dreams were some of the most powerful messages we could receive. It also meant that one was much closer to the spirit world and what you dreamt was more likely to come true. That was a lot to think about.

He didn't have much more time to ponder as he heard Smithson coming back in from his route along the highway.

"You okay, Boss?" asked Smithson. "You look like you've seen a ghost."

"Just a bit tired," said Windflower. "Is everything okay out there?"

"Traffic is pretty busy. People shopping and coming and going for Christmas," said Smithson.

"You're not much of a Christmas person, are you?" asked Windflower.

"Don't really see the point of it all," said Smithson. "My parents split up early, and it seemed to me that Christmas was just a big tug-of-war over me and my sister. We got lots of stuff, but it always felt we were having someone else's Christmas instead of our own. Now, I'd rather work and pick up the overtime. If I had it off, I'd just watch the Star Wars marathon."

"But Christmas is about the spirit of giving and caring, maybe even about hope for love and kindness."

"Well that would be a miracle. I just don't see much evidence to believe in all that."

"Sometimes we have to believe in the miracle before it happens. I'm going to take a couple of hours off and then be back to relieve you. There's lots of food in the fridge."

"That I believe," said Smithson. "See you later."

Windflower drove the short distance home, and when he opened the door of his house, he was greeted by a rush of enthusiasm. Lady, the collie, bounded down the hallway and nearly knocked him over. Molly, the cat, was fast behind her and was soon rubbing up against his leg. He could hear Amelia Louise calling the best words a new father could hear.

"Dada, dada, dada." Over and over again. It would never to be too much for him, and he patted Lady quickly, stroked Molly a few times as she arched her back and then rushed to his daughter's playpen. He grabbed Amelia Louise in his arms and raised her high above his head. She squealed as he shouted, "Daddy's home."

"He most certainly is," said Sheila as she came to join in the fun. Windflower lowered the baby and gave Sheila a big hug and a kiss.

"What is that most delicious smell?" asked Windflower.

"That's the last of my baking," said Sheila. "Spiced molasses lassies. My mom used to make these from a secret recipe she got from her mother. I could give it to you, but then I'd have to kill you. And I kind of like having you around."

"I'd love to try one later once my stomach goes down from our Christmas lunch."

"Everybody get off okay?"

"Yeah, gone their separate ways for the holidays. It's good they left today. I hear we're getting a whack of snow."

"Ah, it'll be nice to have some white stuff at Christmas," said Sheila. "I hear Santa might bring us something to enjoy it with."

"A snowmobile?" Windflower believed in being hopeful.

"Non-mechanical," said Sheila with a chuckle. "Both of us could use the exercise."

"So could Lady by the looks of it," said Windflower, handing the baby back to Sheila.

"You take her out, and I'll start the princess's bath. When you get back you can read her a story."

"That sounds like a deal."

Windflower walked to the kitchen and grabbed Lady's leash. The collie had beaten him to the door and barely waited long enough for him to put on her leash before she was outside.

Windflower loved walking around Grand Bank at

Christmastime. Almost every house had lights and decorations ranging from white twinkle lights, that he didn't really believe were true Christmas lights, to blow-ups of Frosty and Santa and all eight reindeer. It was a kaleidoscope of colours, and many of the outdoor set-ups had music to go along with them. He was humming to himself as he and Lady strolled all over.

As they were turning for home, Windflower felt the wind rise and saw the first snowflakes flutter to the ground. By the time they arrived, both man and dog were covered in a fluffy white blanket. He tried to wipe Lady, but of course she shook herself and her snow all over the kitchen floor where Molly did her best to eat up as much as she could before it melted.

"Thank you, Molly," Windflower said to the cat.

"Who are you talking to?" called Sheila from upstairs.

Windflower pretended he didn't hear that. He didn't really want to say he was having a conversation with the animals. "It's snowing," he replied.

"I know. Isn't it beautiful?"

"It is, as long as we don't get too much of it," said Windflower as he rose the stairs. "Poor Smithson will have to deal with any problems that come up."

"That young man will be fine. Right now, our young lady is ready for her bedtime story."

"It's almost time for *'Twas the Night Before*

Christmas. But tonight it will be *Bear Stays Up for Christmas.*"

Windflower took the book from the shelf and put the freshly washed Amelia Louise in his arms. He sat in the rocking chair and opened the book. The little girl immediately pointed to the bear as if to wake him up.

"That's right, we have to wake up Bear for Christmas," said Windflower.

By the time he had nearly finished the book, Amelia Louise's little eyes were starting to close, and with one big yawn she fell fast sleep. Windflower rocked her for a few more minutes, just because he liked to do that, and then gently laid her in the crib. He kissed her on the cheek and quietly slipped out of the room.

Downstairs Sheila had made appetizers and a small cheese plate, with the obligatory cookie tray for dessert. She had a glass of white wine, while Windflower settled for a cup of tea. The couple spent a few lovely hours chatting and watching the classic Scrooge with Alastair Sim until it was time for Windflower to go and relieve Smithson.

"I'm going over to the Mug-Up in the morning for their Christmas Eve breakfast. Why don't you come over with the baby, if there's not too much snow?"

"I'm from Newfoundland, Sergeant, there's only too much snow when it's over the rooftops. We'll take the sled. See you then. I'll call you in the morning."

Windflower kissed Sheila and patted his pets on the way out the door. There was already enough snow on his Jeep to get the brush and sweep it off. It was fine snow, like dust. Like the kind we could get an awful of, thought Windflower as he drove back to work.

❦

Windflower was right. They were getting a lot of snow. By the time Smithson left for the night, there was a pile already on the ground, and the wind was whipping it up into near whiteout conditions. When Windflower left for his midnight tour of Grand Bank, the streets were snow-covered and getting slippery. He passed the snowplow operator, Evan Shortall, near the edge of town and waved him a goodnight. He might not be getting too much of a break this Christmas either, thought Windflower.

He drove onto the highway and took his time as he guided his Jeep into the path that Shortall had just carved out. Luckily, there were no other cars on the road tonight. It would have made passing each other very difficult. He made it successfully all the way to the turnoff to Creston North, almost into Marystown. Then he pulled over and called into the Marystown RCMP for a weather update.

The news was great for those who had been wishing for a white Christmas. The forecast was for snow, more snow and drifting and blowing snow for at least the next twenty-four hours, maybe longer if the onshore winds persisted. He talked to traffic control and told them that if they needed to close the highway to go ahead. There was no way that he, or more likely Smithson, would be able to get back here to put up the barricades and beacons.

He slowly drove back toward Grand Bank passing the Garnish and Frenchman's Cove exits with little sign of life or activity. There was more to see as he passed by Grand Beach and Molliers with strings of Christmas lights welcoming him back to his neck of the woods. Finally, in the distance he could see the twinkling of the little Town of Grand Bank. He smiled whenever he saw this sight, reminding himself to be grateful for all he had received and all the love that this place held in his heart.

Back at the detachment he made himself a cup of tea and a turkey sandwich, washed down with one of Betsy's homemade jam jams. All was so peaceful and quiet on his watch that he snuck into one of the cells and set the alarm for a half-hour nap. This time there were no dreams, and when the alarm went off, he nudged it back on for another half hour.

The rest of the night went smoothly, and the snow kept piling up. In the morning, Sheila called around seven o'clock to chat and tell him what Amelia Louise had been up to so far. That included trying to eat some of the dog's food before Sheila snatched it away.

She was bundling them both up to head over to the café. Windflower promised to see them soon.

When Smithson arrived at a quarter to eight, the snow had half buried Windflower's Jeep in the parking lot, which the younger Mountie was having difficulty getting into but eventually succeeded.

"Morning, Boss," said Smithson. "I saw Shortall, the snowplow guy, and asked him to clear us off when he gets a chance. He told me that he'll do it before he goes home. He's shutting down except for emergencies after that."

"Yeah, tons of snow," said Windflower. "I told Marystown that they were on their own if they decided to close the highway."

"That's great," said Smithson. "I don't think I could get out there anyway. You can barely get around town. Anything happen overnight?"

"All is calm and bright here," said Windflower. "Hopefully, it'll stay the same for you. If anything happens, give me a call, okay?"

"Sure. But like you said, nothing ever happens in Grand Bank, right?" said Smithson optimistically, if not completely confidently.

"Right," said Windflower. "Now I've got a date with two beautiful girls. So, Merry Christmas, Constable."

"Merry Christmas, Sergeant," said Smithson.

Windflower cleaned off his Jeep and drove to the Mug-Up. Despite the snow and early hour there were eight or nine cars outside the café and Christmas carols blaring from an outside speaker. Inside, the cafe was filled with warmth and laughter and, by the sounds of it, some great Christmas spirit.

Windflower spotted Sheila and Amelia Louise and gave them a wave. He greeted all the other diners along the way and stopped at the kitchen door to call his Merry Christmas in to Moira and Herb Stoodley who were busy cooking and dishing up an enormous quantity of food.

Windflower sat with Sheila and took Amelia Louise in his arms. Herb Stoodley came around with a fresh pot of coffee and then brought Sheila her breakfast; scrambled eggs, homemade beans and toutons with molasses.

"I love toutons," said Windflower as he watched Sheila pour a pool of molasses on her plate and then dip the fried bread delicacy into it. "Hmmmm," she said, partly out of sheer joy and partly to tease her husband.

"You are a cruel woman," said Windflower. He picked a spoonful of scrambled eggs and tried to feed Amelia Louise, but she grabbed the spoon from him and stuffed it in her mouth. "And you're teaching your daughter to be just as bad," he said. Sheila laughed, and Amelia Louise laughed, too.

"See, I told you," said Windflower. He was placated soon after when his plate came along, with the added bonus of a piece of fried bologna. "Thank you, Herb," said Windflower. "At least somebody cares about me."

Sheila laughed again and took the baby in her arms to finish feeding her while Windflower ate his breakfast. Inhaled it was more like it. She looked over at him in astonishment. "Where did your food go?" she asked, pointing to his empty plate.

"That was sum good b'y," said Windflower, rubbing his belly. Amelia Louise rubbed her belly, too. Moira who was coming by to pick up dishes saw the baby and started to laugh.

"She is such a big girl now," said Moira. "Come see your Auntie Moira."

Amelia Louise already had her hands out, and Moira laid down her tray and took the little girl on a tour of the café. Smiles and laughter followed the pair as they traversed the room, and Windflower and Sheila finished their coffee, smiling at all the people cooing to their baby daughter. After visiting everyone, Moira gave Amelia Louise to her husband, Herb, and returned to cleaning up. Herb sat with Windflower and Sheila until the baby's restlessness told everybody it was time to move.

Sheila bundled up the baby, and they said their goodbyes and Merry Christmases all around. The wind almost knocked them over when they opened the café door. They managed to get to Windflower's Jeep, which was covered in snow again. He drove slowly through the only narrow pathway that substituted for a road in Grand Bank, carefully dodging the few brave souls who were trying to get to the café or to Warren's for a last-minute item. Windflower drove past the RCMP offices and could see that Smithson had persuaded the snowplow operator to clear their parking lot. It was the only clean lot in Grand Bank. All the lights were on and Smithson had moved the RCMP snowmobile to the front along with his vehicle. Smart move, thought Windflower. He also thought about stopping in but looked over at a sleeping Amelia Louise and decided to keep going home.

Inside the house Amelia Louise woke up as Sheila took off her snowsuit, and Windflower played with her on the floor until a very impatient Lady nudged him enough to get his attention. He took the dog for a short walk, more of a trudge really. Lady thought the snow was absolutely the most magical thing she had ever seen. She jumped in it, rolled in it and tried to catch it as it fell near her. She finally settled for eating as much as she could. Windflower laughed at her antics and wished he could find so much joy in such a regular occurrence as snow in Newfoundland.

When he got back, Sheila and Amelia Louise and Molly were wrapping presents. Well, Sheila was wrapping. The baby and cat were both trying to crawl into a large empty box. It looked like Molly was winning, until Windflower saw his daughter deftly pull the cat out and insert herself. He happily joined in the fun.

Later that afternoon Sheila put a glazed ham in the oven for their supper while Windflower made his special scalloped potatoes and put them in the fridge. His task complete, he offered to take Amelia Louise up for her nap. Sheila just smiled as the sleepy pair almost skipped upstairs. She could hear Windflower reading a story and soft sounds from the baby. Then nothing.

Windflower fell into a deep and relaxing sleep. Then he woke up – in his dream. He was back in the snow and as his eyes adjusted, he could see shadows in the distance again. Instead of approaching, he stood as still as possible and held out his arms to the side of him. That would show whoever or whatever was out there that he posed no danger. He tried to stay quiet and to breathe as softly as possible. He could see his breath rise in the cold air and started to notice the figures come closer, very slowly. This was good; they were curious, he thought.

When they were about fifteen feet in front of him, he saw the two deer. It looked like the female from his last dream and a large male deer with solid shoulders and antlers. As they drew closer, he realized that the male was actually a reindeer.

Windflower understood the deer spirit. It was part of his family's teachings that deer were not just wild animals or food to be hunted but messengers from the spirit world who would help humans if they were asked. The male deer were known as the kings of the forest, and the fact that they had antlers meant that they were closer to the sky than other animals. Reindeer had special honours and privileges in the animal world because they had learned to survive in a harsh northern climate. Windflower had never seen a reindeer, except in the movies or on television. This felt like a powerful omen to him. He decided to ask why they had visited him in his dreamworld.

"Why are you here?" he asked.

The smaller one snorted and started to walk away, but the reindeer stood staring at him. "We have already brought you a message, but you have chosen to ignore it."

"What do you mean?" asked Windflower. "I am looking after my little one, my daughter."

"Not all little ones are babies, and some of us are innocent. Wisdom is not just learning, but experience," said the reindeer. Now he was walking away, too.

"Wait," said Windflower. "I don't understand." Then he saw another one, this time a young, maybe a male, deer in the background near the forest. That one looked directly at him and then followed the others into the forest. The snow swirled frantically, and Windflower woke up.

So did Amelia Louise, and Windflower went to change her and put her into a fancy dress that Sheila had laid out for her to wear on Christmas Eve. The aromas from downstairs nearly drove Windflower mad.

"That ham smells gorgeous," he called down to Sheila.

"Come down and I'll feed the baby, and then we'll have our dinner," she called back.

"I have to make a quick call," said Windflower. "I'm a bit worried about Smithson."

"Everything okay over there?" asked Windflower when Smithson answered the phone.

"All good," said Smithson. "We had a couple of calls asking about the highway. I guess some people were trying to get back for Christmas. But I told them that Marystown had closed the road after lunch. Other than that, all is quiet on the RCMP front."

"Excellent," said Windflower. "If you need me for anything, just call, okay?"

"I will," said Smithson. "But I'm not anticipating any problems, Sir."

Windflower almost said, "That's when they come, when we least expect them," but instead simply said, "Merry Christmas," and he hung up.

"Everything okay?" asked Sheila as she wiped a streak of mushy scalloped potatoes off Amelia Louise's chin.

"So far so good," said Windflower. "But I think I'll skip the wine tonight. I have a feeling that something is going to happen. I can pour you a glass though."

"No. You know what I'd like to drink. Purity syrup with some Perrier in it. We always had strawberry syrup mixed with water on Christmas Eve. This'll be like a fancy version."

Windflower mixed their drinks and then took the baby from Sheila so she could dish up their dinner. The maple glazed ham looked delicious, and when Sheila cut into it, Windflower's eyes started to water in anticipation. She put two thick slices on his plate along with a small portion of meat from the crispy outside, which she knew he loved, scooped up a generous portion of scalloped potatoes and a ladle of broccoli and put it in front of him.

He cooled off a small piece of broccoli and let Amelia Louise have it while he started to tuck into his dinner. All Sheila heard for the next few minutes was "mmmmmmmm" from Windflower and something similar but less intelligible from the baby. She was happy to have a little break to enjoy her Christmas Eve dinner in peace.

Windflower finished his plate and handed it back to Sheila for a refill. He cleaned the baby up and put her in her playpen before settling down again to enjoy his seconds.

"Man, that's good," he said when he finally came up for air.

"It's nice to have a ham for Christmas Eve," said Sheila. "We always had that at home with Mom and Dad. Then we'd go to the midnight vigil at church. We'd have our turkey dinner the next day at lunchtime."

"That would be great," said Windflower. "But I'm glad we're waiting until Boxing Day to have our turkey. I don't think I can eat again for a few days."

"I'm sure your appetite will pick up again," said Sheila. "If you clean up, I'll go give our little lady a bath. Then we can hang up our stockings."

"Super," said Windflower. "I'll pop Lady out in the back, too."

Sheila went upstairs, and he could hear her singing over the running water. He opened the back door and was surprised by how much snow had accumulated on the deck. He had to force the door a little and grabbed a shovel to clear a path for Lady to get out and down the stairs. The dog looked a little puzzled at this approach, but finally figured it out and scrambled down the steps. She came back in a few minutes, looking both relieved and a bit disappointed that a walk didn't seem to be in the offing. Windflower shrugged and brought her indoors to wipe her down.

A Milk Bone biscuit seemed to pacify her, as did a special treat for Molly who knew that she deserved at least that.

Windflower cleaned everything up and was waiting in the living room near the Christmas tree when Sheila came down with the baby in her Christmas pyjamas. They took turns taking pictures, including both pets who demanded to be in every shot, then hung up all three stockings on the mantle. Windflower then took Amelia Louise in his arms and sat beside Sheila on the couch.

She got 'Twas the Night Before Christmas out and handed it to him. Amelia Louise loved the story, especially the beginning about the mouse who, in this version, appeared on just about every page. Molly was interested in the mouse, too, although maybe she was just angling for another treat while Lady was curled up contentedly, sleeping on her master's feet.

When the story was over, Sheila took the baby upstairs for one more feeding and then rocked her to sleep. The couple had tea and a tray of cookies, which Windflower managed to mostly eat, despite his apparent lack of appetite. They watched It's a Wonderful Life, and both cried a little at the end, as always. Windflower said goodnight to both pets and made sure they had clean water and food before turning out the lights on the Christmas tree and following Sheila upstairs to bed.

That night, there were no more dreams for Windflower, and at precisely six o'clock Amelia Louise woke them as if to wish them a Merry Christmas. Windflower got up, changed the baby and handed her back to her mother. He padded downstairs and put the coffee on while Lady took a brief trip outside. Speaking of outside, it was still snowing and blowing, and when Windflower looked out his front door, he could see that the drifting snow had made the roads virtually impassable.

He let the dog in, and while both pets circled his feet, he made his smudge bowl and sat in front of the Christmas tree. He lit the mixture of herbs and offered his prayers of thanks to the morning and to Creator for all the gifts he had received and those that he knew were on the way. He prayed for those who might be alone or troubled this Christmas morning, and he prayed that his family and friends would receive the support they need for their journeys.

He packed his smudge kit away and went to the back porch where he had hidden Sheila's Christmas roses. He gathered them carefully in his arms and went upstairs. "Merry Christmas, everybody," he said as he handed Sheila her flowers and took the baby in return.

"Merry Christmas, Winston. The flowers are beautiful. Thank you," said Sheila. She reached over to give him a kiss. "Let's go and see if Santa came last night."

Amelia Louise laughed to indicate she was ready and soon all of them were sitting on the floor under the tree with pets and presents everywhere. Amelia Louise and the cat were most interested in the wrapping paper and bows. Lady had somehow found her present, a package of dried bones, and had already managed to open the package. She had all of them in her mouth before Windflower pulled it away. It was a scene of a happy family's Christmas joy.

Then Windflower's cell phone rang.

"Boss, it's me," said Smithson. "Sorry to bother you. But we've got a situation."

"What's going on?" asked Windflower.

"I got a call from young Levi Parsons. He was over at a girl's house, Melissa Sinnott. I'm here and she's pregnant and she thinks she's ready to have the baby," said Smithson, all in one run-on sentence.

"Can you get her to the clinic?" asked Windflower.

"I came over on my snowmobile. You can't get around most of the roads. I called paramedics, but they're out on another call past Grand Beach. Shortall and the snowplow are with them." Windflower could tell Smithson was more than a little anxious.

"How's the girl?" he asked.

"She's pretty nervous. I'd say she's only sixteen, maybe seventeen."

"Is her mother there?"

"She's here but incapacitated at the moment. Drunk and passed out by the looks of it."

"Has her water broke yet?" asked Windflower.

He could hear Smithson ask the girl and then come back on. "Yes, about an hour ago."

"Okay," said Windflower. "Hang on a sec." He laid down the phone and turned to Sheila.

"Remember that year of nursing you did years ago? Did they go over childbirth by any chance?"

"Yes, but that was a long time ago," said Sheila. "Is someone having a baby?"

Windflower filled her in on what he knew and then put the phone on speaker.

"Sheila has some training in nursing; she's going to help you," said Windflower.

Sheila took over from there. She talked first to the girl and calmed her down. The contractions were coming faster now, and she panted as the pain went through her. Sheila spoke to Levi and got him to hold Melissa's hand and let her squeeze it when the next contraction came. She sent Smithson to find some clean towels.

The contractions kept coming as Sheila spoke to the girl. She got Levi to help her lay down and remove her pants and underclothing. The girl was starting to scream now, and Sheila helped her focus on breathing through the pain. If she was right, it wouldn't be long now. She was right, and just as she got Smithson positioned between the girl's legs, he started to almost scream as well.

"I can see the head," he shouted.

"That's good," said Sheila as calmly as she could, hoping it would rub off on Smithson. It did a little, but who it really helped was Levi. He could be heard quietly reassuring the soon-to-be mother that things were going to be okay.

"It's coming, the baby is coming," shouted Smithson some more

This time Sheila didn't bother trying to calm anybody down. The girl screamed, and the next sound that they heard was Smithson shouting, "It's a boy! It just rolled right into my towel. A baby boy."

"Clean the baby off. Is it breathing?" asked Sheila.

"Yes, I think so," said Smithson. "Yes, he's breathing. I'm wiping him off now."

"Wrap him in another towel and hand the baby to the mother now," said Sheila.

Smithson did as told, and everything became very quiet as the mother saw her baby for the first time.

Calmly and quietly Sheila told Smithson to stay where he was with a towel ready because there was still more. A few minutes later, Smithson confidently scooped up the placenta.

"I'm going to get cleaned up," he announced.

Sheila handed the phone back to Windflower and sat back on the couch. She picked up Amelia Louise and held her in her arms. Windflower mouthed a "thank you" to Sheila and blew her a kiss.

Smithson came back on the phone. "I'm back," he said. "I just got a text saying that both the ambulance and the snowplow are on their way. I'll stay here until they get here. In any case, baby and mother and father are doing well."

"He's not the father," said Windflower. "I'll explain later. But congratulations, Constable. You just helped deliver the first Christmas baby in Grand Bank this year."

"Thanks to Sheila," said Smithson.

"Absolutely," said Windflower. "But you showed grace under fire and managed to do the right thing, including calling for help. You now have another experience to add to your arsenal and a great story to tell every Christmas. Maybe you should call it the Christmas miracle."

"It is a miracle, that's for sure," said Smithson. "Merry Christmas, Boss, to you and yours."

"Merry Christmas, Rick. Enjoy the rest of your day. I'll see you after noon." Windflower heard happy sounds in the background as Smithson hung up. When he looked around, he saw happy faces and wagging tales.

"Well, Sheila, that wasn't the Christmas morning we had planned," he said.

"But wasn't it the perfect Christmas morning,

celebrating the birth of a child?" she responded.

"It was and is. You know nothing ever happens in Grand Bank. But when it does, it is almost always something spectacular."

"Like a miracle."

"Like all of this," Windflower agreed as he gestured toward the dog and cat and baby, all engaged in a tug of war over a red bow with a long string of ribbon attached. "Like a Christmas miracle."

About the Author

 Mike Martin was born in Newfoundland on the East Coast of Canada and now lives and works in Ottawa, Ontario. He is a long-time freelance writer and his articles and essays have appeared in newspapers, magazines and online across Canada as well as in the United States and New Zealand. He is the author of *Change the Things You Can: Dealing with Difficult People* and has written a number of short stories that have published in various publications including *Canadian Stories* and *Downhome* magazine.

The Walker on the Cape was his first full fiction book and the premiere of the Sgt. Windflower Mystery Series. Other books in the series include *The Body on the T, Beneath the Surface, A Twist of Fortune* and *A Long Ways from Home*, which was shortlisted for the Bony Blithe Light Mystery Award as the best light mystery of the year. *A Tangled Web* was released in 2017 and the newest book in the series, *Darkest Before the Dawn* won the Bony Blithe Light Mystery Award.

Fire, Fog and Water will be released in October 2019.

Mike is currently Chair of the Board of Crime Writers of Canada, a national organization promoting Canadian crime and mystery writers.

You can follow the Sgt. Windflower Mysteries on Facebook at https://www.facebook.com/TheWalkerOnTheCapeReviewsAndMore/

Printed in Great Britain
by Amazon